TINA AG

SMILING DEPRESSION

A diverse range of compelling short stories

Smiling Depression

First published in Australia byTina Agassiz 2020
www.tinaagassiz.com

NATIONAL LIBRARY OF AUSTRALIA

A catalogue record for this
book is available from the
National Library of Australia

ISBN: 978-0-6489979-0-0 (pbk)
ISBN: 978-0-6489979-1-7 (ebk)

Typesetting and design by Publicious Book Publishing
Published in collaboration with Publicious Book Publishing
www.publicious.com.au

Disclaimer

The material in this publication comes from life experience, from people who have faced adversities that have led them down emotionally dark and depressing avenues and are in the process of reaching greater emotional contentment, having successfully reached deep within themselves to deal with varied causes of life-changing events.

This book is not intended to provide specific guidance for particular circumstances and should not be relied on as grounds for any decisions, including actions or inactions individuals may or may not take. Readers should obtain professional advice where appropriate and before reaching concrete resolutions.

Warning

This book contains content you might find offensive, and is not suitable for some reader audiences. Accordingly, reader discretion is advised and the choice to proceed is viewed as an agreement of accountability. If you proceed past this message, then you alone are accountable for how you react to the content you find.

≈

In this book, important life lessons emerge from the daily reality everyday people face through adversity, fear, anguish, and rejection, leading to the diabolical paralysis of emotional and mental state of mind that leads to emotional disarray, anxiety and depression.

While each story has been designed to gain your attention, the identities of those in this book have been purposely left out to protect individual privacy.

Each story has the potential to move you emotionally as you feel the indelible marks left on the storytellers and their invaluable and thought-provoking life lessons.

The power of positive thinking can change your life forever. Every person has the opportunity to find empowerment to overcome mental, emotional, physical and spiritual barriers.

Each story will teach you to appreciate the life you have if you don't already, and to savour the joy of living every day in a positively infectious way.

Contents

Preface

You are a miracle.

Your first miracle is your birth. The second miracle is when you lose yourself within today's society, lost among the masses before finding yourself again. You suddenly give up your current life by giving your heart to God, and in doing so you become a born-again Christian.

If you want to move past obstacles that hold you back, that you believe are insurmountable, you need to build a sacred relationship with the Holy Spirit and learn what the love of God feels like, particularly if you've never felt his spirit before.

To seek spiritual awakening, to break free of chains and the weight of burdens holding you down, you need to learn to understand the miraculous power of God.

Be transformed today, and not singularly by the writings inside this book, but by the writings of the Holy Bible, and pray. Ask for forgiveness and salvation. Speak your truth and let God know what you need for your life, and assure him you will practice what you preach.

Be saved today and open your heart to God. Allow God to show you the righteous way.

"Smiling Depression"

In this book you will find a diverse range of emotionally compelling stories, shared through a collaborative effort to encourage you to appreciate your own life, if you don't already.

The overall aim is to inform you that you are not alone, to inspire you to live authentically and intrinsically, to live out your best life after breaking through barriers that hold you back or have held you down from becoming the best, most authentic version of yourself.

Like it or not, there will always be pivotal, life-changing moments that will force movement or encourage us to grow, while understanding that each individual is different and for some, life-changing moments can fracture a life forever.

Life catastrophes can break the spirit, especially when an individual fixates their mind on what *was* rather than what is. All their energy and efforts remain constant in trying to recapture past experiences, reminiscing over the way life used to be, rather than what life is now.

Constant thinking of the past and wishing past experiences existed within the now disables forward movement. There's a strong difference between thinking of the past and trying to relive it or living in it. Some enjoy living in the past, especially if the past consists of happier memories. Often those same people would rather live there because thinking about it provides comfort and happiness. This is what I refer to as Time Warp Zones, areas from the past that we wish we could live in.

If you find yourself clinging to a specific period of the past because you don't feel there is anything worthwhile in the present that could improve your life for the better, and you've lost your sense of worth because you feel stuck, sad, lost, anxious or depressed, you are simply robbing yourself of any opportunity to enjoy life and experience happiness again.

Action creates change, not inspiration on its own. Inspiration has a short shelf life without any application to action. Because of this one realisation, each of us needs to focus on concrete practices that lead to sharper focus, improved self-productivity and better collaboration. Without some type of belonging to an affiliated group of people who share similar values and foresight, we can lose our sense of worth, and small problems can become bigger problems. Personal growth begins when we decide enough is enough, and that we are bigger than our problems.

Life is tough, and anyone who ever said it
wasn't simply lied to you.
We don't have to ameliorate our quality
of life. We all have that choice.

Understanding factors or root causes that contribute to growth blockages will help you to source preventative measures and mitigate the impact as you learn to exercise control when needing to rid yourself of all things that encumber you.

Nothing in life stays the same forever. No living being is immune from life happenings, good, bad, happy or sad. Bad things happen to everyone at different stages throughout each of our lives, and it doesn't matter what end of the food chain we belong to. There is no escaping tumultuous upheaval. Things change and new challenges arise, or we may seek out new challenges as a way to manifest self-growth. Challenges ought to be constant, never stagnant, because life without challenges is ineffectual, pointless and meaningless.

The pain of life, in all its forms, is inevitable—it's part of being human.

Mission Statement

To enable greatness in individual people and to help unleash the power within so you may focus on the priority of living and flourish vigorously in self-worth.

Vision Statement

Using my strengths to serve others, to help all levels of readers to achieve fulfilment, no matter the challenges being faced, and thereby enriching not only their life but the community that surrounds them.

My Values

All people, adults and young children, should live a life free from abuse and neglect.
No child should be marginalised or made to feel worthless, not wanted or inept.
Everyone should have the opportunity to actively participate in all facets of life, especially where it involves self-worth and belonging.
Focusing on individual assets and strengths leads to success eventually.
All things we decide to do are ethical, fair and provided in a manner of integrity, compassion and competence, even if we should lack a little in confidence.

By realising your potential, you are creating hope and building on your future. Your footprint leaves an invaluable mark for generations after you.

Dedication

This book was written in honour of those who've suffered, whether as children or adults.

To all who've been marginalised, neglected, battered, abused, and made to feel inept. To any person who has been violated, bullied, victimised, traumatised, and who, like me and others in this book, have always dreamed of a better life with an ontological perspective of knowing that each of us deserves to find peace, to live peacefully, and for lost happiness to be restored.

There is one thing that doubt doesn't like; it's the
way we become determined to prove it wrong.

Life is like a fire torch. The light shines brightly, illuminating our pathway until the flame burns out. It can be hard to keep the fire burning over the years, but it is up to us to reignite the flame and keep it burning.

In keeping the flame burning we need to ensure a connectable effort is made. A connectable effort needs to be our primary focus and therefore requires us to undergo various transformative redesigns to increase resilience that is less likely to burn out.

There is always room for limitless creativity.

Successful individuals keep their fire torch burning even when the flame seems dim.

I have dedicated my life to sharing my symbolic
flame, transferred person to person, elaborately
and brightly, no matter what part
of the world they reside in.

Introduction

Fate landed me with an alcoholic woman, my adoptive mother, who partied most of her life away while collecting the sole parent benefit every fortnight from Work and Income, provided by the New Zealand government.

When I look back on my childhood experiences, I realise the many lessons I have learnt. I'm ever so grateful I've turned out the way I have, and it's thanks to my grandmother and my love for God.

As a pure and innocent little girl, after reading *My Book of Bible Stories* I knew there was something different in me. I also realised the lack of connectedness to many of those within my own family, apart from my grandmother.

I struggled to relate to various happenings that surrounded me for most of my childhood, especially the partying, where high volumes of alcohol were often consumed. I hated walking into my own home to find drunken adults sitting around the kitchen table, smoking cigarettes, and talking obnoxiously loudly over party music whilst sipping or sculling back bottles of beer.

All I wanted was to have peace in my own home, to feel comfortable in my own space so I could concentrate on imagining what my life might look like if it didn't look like that.

I understand that exploiting my feelings and childhood experiences may make me vulnerable, endangering my peaceful serenity with the chance of ridicule. But I feel I have long cared enough for myself and have learnt to protect and love myself in every which way I can, so I'm ready for the possibility of hate speeches and intense dislike from those who've never liked or loved me. I'm preparing for the odium, which causes their version, and is something I have distanced myself from for most of my adult life.

Life is like a battlefield.
Some come prepared to die. Few come
prepared to live.

My life has felt like war, although without large tanks and heavy artillery. So many times over the years I have found my back against a wall. I've had to fight like hell for most things.

Some things stand out in abusive perpetrators, such as jealousy, controlling, unreasonable and manipulative behaviours, substance abuse, explosive tempers with threats of violence, just to name a few. I often felt my adoptive mother was jealous of me, as were members of my own family. I've been dealing with jealousy and manipulative and unreasonable behaviours my entire life. At high school, in many of my workplaces and in my past relationship there were similar problems. It seemed everywhere I turned my back was up against a wall, face-to-face with abusive perpetrators who had serious problems but didn't see it the same way I did.

In my adult life I learnt to walk away, even if it meant losing my livelihood.

I will always stand by my innermost values at all costs because they've helped me to live authentically, and more importantly, are of ecclesiastical distinction. As an adult, I believe that valued-based decisions are what design the future and that my inner values are not limited to one individual's personal beliefs. Strong values hold universally fundamental quality, and fundamental quality itself is hard to beat. Thank God for saving me.

≈

So how do I get to the place I want to go with my back up against a wall more often than not? I get there through awareness and being present to life as I am living it. That means to feel the full experience of what I am doing and knowing my why, and savouring each moment, believing that someone, somewhere in the world, will appreciate my words now and in the future. That is my catalyst, and I feel comfortable with that.

I've learnt that when I believe in myself, an idea, or my life project, nothing can make me forget the efforts I have made to achieve such goals. Whilst situations can sometimes be complicated for me to manage, there is often a positive outcome in my case.

With the leg work I'm doing now, and with a singular focus of helping people through God's language and writing, I feel that in the up-and-coming years I'll be able to express myself and make my opinion valued. I believe opportunities will arise that will broaden life's horizons so I can continue to help others achieve their dreams.

Positive Affirmations

The world of thoughts that you reside in creates your reality. That means that every fear, hope, dream and negative or hostile provoking thought that makes its way through your mind has an impact on your life.

There are times we all reach a point of intense thinking of a negative kind. Negative thinking can manifest itself like wildfire, rapidly and powerfully if you allow it. Negativity is a force to be reckoned with. When you learn how to handle it, you'll turn a negative situation into a positive one. When losing control of good thoughts, refocus and replace the negative thoughts with positive, hopeful and benevolent ones. It might take a fair amount of will and commitment to do this and to keep doing it, but if you can, you will soon see a dramatic improvement in the way you feel, see, and relate to the world.

Life can be a feast if you look for the beauty that surrounds you and allow it to nourish your soul, so feast your eyes on the beauty in your world and let it replenish you.

It takes a long time to evolve. No matter the age, or how much we think we know or have learnt, we are still evolving. If we remain open-minded, we will continue to evolve throughout the rest of our lives.

Sometimes we are hard on ourselves for not knowing more, not making the best decisions, and so on. But we need to recognise that as long as we are doing our best, then that is the best we can do.

When we make mistakes, we may start to blame ourselves for some missed chance or error of judgement. Be patient, all things turn around eventually and wonderfully, restoring faith once lost.

Sometimes a fond memory from long ago is coloured and brightened by a sense of nostalgia. Human beings tend to filter out the rough spots, the hurt feelings or regrets that occurred. But that's okay, because when we look back happily into the past we aspire to achieve the same kind of happiness in the present moment. It is possible to recreate something beautiful from the past, we just need to find the inspiration, the purpose and the way to do so.

Sometimes we can take a cynical approach to many things in life because we are afraid of being hurt, rejected or taken advantage of. Yes, it is wise to be cautious, but being too cautious or cynical can make life dull and can lead to a lack of happiness. It is wise to approach new things with caution, but more rewarding when we approach things in a childlike way with a sense of hope and wonder. We can still protect ourselves even if we adopt this outlook, and it will be more amendable to a happy outcome.

In an era where manual labour was relied on over machinery, before a miner struck gold or diamonds, they often had a huge amount of digging to do. Their efforts involved separating what was unnecessary from what was essential. There are areas in our lives that can benefit significantly from this method. By addressing what is superfluous from what's integral the equivalent of a gold nugget or diamond waits to be discovered.

Throwing in the proverbial towel is always easy to consider when we make an effort and don't see immediate results. There'll be times you'll wonder if you're pursuing a life-long pipeline or something that's going to take too long to come to fruition. Do not underestimate your belief levels or what a bit more faith and effort can bring. Proof that you're not wasting your time or effort will come. Remain strong to your inner faith and faith will reward you kindly.

Glamour magazines dwell in the land of fantasy. Even the most beautiful models in the world are always photoshopped and airbrushed to perfection. Avoid dwelling on perceived flaws about yourself. Instead, focus on all the fine qualities that make you who you are as a whole. Through complete acceptance and love you will find true perfection.

Throughout history, countless brilliant ideas that were initially mocked and laughed at later proved to be successful. Remember that some people just can't envision the possibilities for a brilliant idea until they see it manifest. Don't give up on your ideas. Validation will come when you remain persistent.

Rarely do we invest effort without having a result in mind. Given that thought precedes every action we take, we either consciously or unconsciously visualize the desired outcome. Sometimes all we want is a subtle indication that we're doing something right and are also right to continue trying. Then there are the times we receive an unexpected or surprising result. When you believe in the talents you have, anything is possible.

Some situations may seem more bad than good, but that may be because we focus more on the problem rather than on a solution. In doing so we are overlooking all the good that is also inherent in the situation. When problems arise, we need to look at them constructively, not critically. Doing so will enable us to find a happy solution.

As children, we learn to focus on whatever or whoever provides the most immediate security. As we grow older, people and items become replaced. Then we reach a point in our world where we become aware of something we've outgrown and why the time has come to release ourselves from it. When we reach a new sense of nostalgia, an appropriate form of emotional security is coming.

Letting go of what other people think is embracing and accepting who you are. People can sometimes feel threatened when you change your lifestyle or turn your own life around. The reality is, it highlights what they don't want to change in themselves, preferring the old you who hangs out and does what they do. There'll be times when you'll receive unsupportive comments or smart remarks trying to push you off your path. In such situations, connect to your inner will and your values and be decisive with your choices.

Life Experience, People and Stories

While we may not earn ourselves a considerable living, and we may not earn ourselves an income from what we love to do, it is within our power to try to leave behind an invaluable blueprint for years after our time.

About the Author

(Tina, age 40)

I come from a dysfunctional, poverty-stricken family where alcoholism, abuse and violence existed. Denied by my biological mother before birth, and by my biological father before and after birth, I was neglected, marginalised and made to feel useless and inept by my alcoholic, narcissistic adoptive mother.

In my earliest years I was raised by a narcissistic woman who drank heavily most days and condemned me for existing. She did, however, happily receive welfare payments from the New Zealand government for as long as I lived in her care and under her roof (technically the house was owned by Housing New Zealand).

I grew up in Selwyn Heights, Rotorua, from the late '70s to the late '80s. A medium decile area, it has deteriorated significantly over time. Some of our old neighbours still reside in their own homes and have no interest in moving. Although I am glad to have moved on from there, whenever I'm in New Zealand and visiting the area I call in for a visit to see how they're doing, or at least drive through the old streets and reflect on old memories.

At four years old, I spent a lot of time amusing myself on the back doorstep after a day of kindergarten. I'd arrive home to a locked-up house with no way in. Even though I grew up in a time where we were fortunate enough to have friendly and kind neighbours, most of the time I was too shy to knock on their door and ask for warmth, food and comfort.

With the sun down and the moon rising, I'd often sit on the back doorstep finding things to do to help pass time while feeling cold and hungry. I'd find old preservative glass jars with lids and catch spiders, moths, bees and wasps. Sometimes I'd make daisy chains or simply weed the gardens. I also remember paying special attention to the praying mantis insect, fascinated by its front legs that looked as if it was praying before or after its hunt. I'd watch for what seemed like hours, observing its body parts and movements while finding its bright green colour somewhat appealing. I remember playing with ants, not to hurt them, but to lead them back to their nest. Now I see how, as a child, I'd find simple things to observe and do to pass the time.

Locked out of my own home and feeling excessively thirsty, I'd drink water from the garden hose, despite it tasting like rubbery plastic. When hunger pains became too much to bear, I'd pull honeysuckles from the tree that sat neatly beside our backdoor step. I'd bite the ends of each honeysuckle, sucking the flavour of honey from each. Well, I think it was honey. It tasted very much like honey and I never felt sick afterwards.

On other occasions I'd eat sweet grass straight from the garden, or depending on the season, I'd pick fruit from our trees, and sometimes the neighbour's, hoping they wouldn't see me.

I remember falling to sleep on the back doorstep on various occasions, to be woken by my drunk adoptive mother as she unlocked the door. She knew full-well she had locked me out of the house and I'd be sitting or sleeping on the back doorstep, cold, hungry and alone, but she never seemed to care. She'd give no apologies for leaving me alone and locked out of my own home. After all, it was my home to live in as much as hers.

She wasn't one to go to work, nor did she have any business sense to create a sustainable income. My adoptive mother was known to collect her fortnightly solo parent benefit and pay the rent, purchase alcohol, smoke, and party away the rest of the money with her drunken family members and friends. That was pretty much my life in her 'care,' with or without her violent and verbally abusive boyfriends.

My household and childhood were riddled with negativity. Things got worse when my younger brother was adopted. His birth mother was my adopted older sister, but she wasn't in any condition to mother a child and was diagnosed with schizophrenia. When I look back on that now, I don't believe she was diagnosed correctly. That said, my adoptive mother wasn't exactly a shining example of what a loving mother ought to have been, she was hardly ever coherent enough to look after anyone. On the days she was sober, the love she said she felt was fabrication and lies.

A little while after my adopted brother came along, I remember spending a lot of time with my grandparents. They owned their house and kept an immaculate home inside and out. I loved it with my grandparents, especially my grandmother, who I often referred to as Nanny. She always made me feel welcome and I never went without.

My grandfather was a heavy drinker and a chain smoker. I don't know if he was always that way inclined or if his habits came about after the accident that meant he couldn't work anymore. I don't recall him being at home much. He'd often walk down to the local pub and return home when he was good and ready. My grandfather was a harmless man. He never raised his voice and he was always loving toward me, but I never fully bonded with him because a little while later he died. He got gangrene in his left leg and it spread quite rapidly. He ended up in the hospital and was told his leg had to be amputated. The operation was a success, but my grandfather made a quiet decision to take his own life when no one was looking. Word got around that he undid his bandages, removed his stitches and bled to death. Family members said doctors and nurses had done all their checks. I guess my grandfather calculated his move causing his death. I have often wondered if he was quietly suffering from depression after the accident that prevented him from ever working again.

My grandmother was a quality woman who never touched alcohol and never smoked. A mother of twenty-two children, she kept a clean and presentable home with immaculate gardens and trimmed hedging and cooked every day. There was food on the table morning, afternoon and night.

I remember her daily habits. Upon waking in the morning she'd make the bed, then wash and freshen herself up before making an effort on her appearance. She'd moisturise her face with Olay before doing her hair in rollers, placing a scarf over her head and dressing conservatively, then head to the kitchen and start making breakfast for whoever was staying in the house. Nanny was a loving woman, a housewife, and you'd never hear her speak a bad word about anyone.

She owned a black and white patchy looking cat called Smokey. He'd follow her everywhere she went, and when Nanny went to housie (also known as bingo), he'd somehow know what time to expect her back and wait at the front gate, laying on the concrete fence right beside Nanny's beautiful rose gardens.

Visiting my grandparents were the days I treasured and enjoyed the most as a kid. My grandmother lived for several years after my grandfather died, but shortly after his death their home was placed on the market with a sign out the front saying 'For Sale.' My grandmother ended up living with an aunt and lived a fairly decent life, dying a little after I turned seventeen and was pregnant with my first child.

I miss my grandmother the most. She was quite the woman, and in her company as a little girl I learnt what it meant to have traditional values. To me, she was the beginning of the rest of my life.

Short Summary

I have longed nurtured myself to develop my spirituality, traditional values and my love for God, to show gratitude for my every day, giving praise to the heavens above in appreciation of the gifts and talents the heavens have provided me with. I have learned to recite in positivity upon awakening each day, placing thankfulness as my priority before commencing wholeheartedly in my calling, and you can do the same.

We must live life learning to:

- Eradicate old wounds by learning to accept ourselves.
- Accept what was and what is.
- To grieve over life losses, acknowledge and express.
- To seek closure on all impedes, blockages and setbacks.

- Alter the mindset, recognising that we can't go back, we can only go forward.
- To change our perspective as it ages, and to overcome all shame and silence the inner critic.

Doing away with irrational beliefs of not
feeling good enough is rewarding.

"I am more than good enough."

Breakthrough

In times of hardship you will find yourself either growing stronger in resilience or weighed down in silence. Resolve can be found in both, though that's not to say you won't have days where you feel less enthusiastic about particular events, goals and dreams.

Overall, you won't feel as if you're doing it all on your own with an endearing voice in the background telling you to *never give up, there are many great things yet to come.*

When you find your purpose in life, you will find strength and understanding. When you know what purpose means to you, the light within you will shine upon those who need it most. You will clearly and instinctively tap into the power of strength, recognising self-worth.

If you're someone who loves to help others and is struggling to find the right pavements to build a pathway to your future, my best suggestion is this:

Learn how to use inevitable difficulties of
the past as a catalyst to create something
so much more empowering.

Delight others through your life experience. As per the adage—you must first understand to be understood. Friendships blossom from such a catalyst and life is transformed within such moments.

May your life begin to shine brightly and wonderfully.

Colossians 3:15-17

And let the peace of Christ rule in your hearts, to which indeed you were called in one body. And be thankful. Let the word of Christ dwell in you richly, teaching and admonishing one another in all wisdom, singing psalms and hymns and spiritual songs, with thankfulness in your hearts to God. And whatever you do, in word or deed, do everything in the name of the Lord Jesus, giving thanks to God the Father through him.

Confirmation Message

For most of my life I had to put up with my adoptive mother and family members who've criticised me, made cynical remarks and ridiculed my being. At high school I was picked on, made fun of and bullied. In workplaces I've been treated poorly and even ignored by superiors. My work ethic and punctuality were unquestionable, but my talents deemed never good enough.

Was it because I wasn't one for greasing up to my managers, rather someone who'd work quietly and tenaciously in the background to get the job done? For the most part, I didn't feel all that comfortable forming close-knit relationships with my managers, even though I held respect for many of them. For one, my profession always landed me in male-dominated work environments.

Looking back on my professional life, white-collar environments tend to have preconceived ideas of how individuals ought to work. Office life was often dense, serious and horrifically boring, and anyone would think laughing was a crime. Overall, white-collar environments just didn't suit my spiritual being, even though I was good at what I did.

During my life I've been able to develop benchmark values to hold on to. Now I feel the need to reach my full potential by following my own set of principles and my moral compass, respecting the most important thing in my life, which is life.

I consider myself one of those people today's society encounters all too rarely, who can look past things and seek to understand with meaning and value. I seek testament over all things, keeping a listening ear, sharing empathy, understanding, and sometimes providing counsel when needed. I sincerely hope that whatever loved ones I have left appreciate me for those qualities, including my sensitivity, sharing my clear-sightedness and my singular way of thinking, as well as the way I look at the world. Whilst I have shared a lot of empathy, I have been known for my straight-down-the-line approach with those I love significantly. The more clarity and wide-eyed my vision, the firmer I become. Admittedly, I tend to come down hard on those

I sincerely love. It's not to hurt their feelings, but is intended to provide reality checks, often on hearing excuses being made for inappropriate behaviour and life happenings.

To me, my qualities are not simply great, but can be regarded as significantly valuable ones that I hope someday promise a good life, and not just for me, but all who have known me and surround me.

In my faith, I hope to illuminate my future by being myself and remaining consistent with my values. I hope to find myself completely fulfilled in sharing with others what others do not share with me. For me, this is a long-awaited prolific period of life where everything is in its place, where I can finally blossom beside the people who can see me as a good and deserving person, and those who sincerely matter to me. To herald a prosperous life full of happiness and success has been a lifetime dream.

I place my truths and my heart on the line in the hope of making significant strides in my life by relinquishing the burdens of my childhood past. I want to live out the rest of my days helping people, to deliver windows of hope and spiritual awakenings filled with emotional substance, to encourage, and to provide faith to those who so desperately need it.

1
Wave Goodbye

(Nathaniel, age 45)

I was sexually abused by our local catholic priest, a man my mother and I had placed our trust in.

I was about six years old when the sexual abuse began. My mother would drop me around to the home belonging to our catholic priest, believing, as did I, that I'd learn about God and the role of an altar boy.

Mum and Dad had separated and agreed to divorce by that point in my life. I didn't have a father figure to rely on after that and I didn't get to see my dad much, if at all. Dad disappeared for most of my childhood, leaving me with my mum and younger siblings. Mum did her best to raise us, well that's what I believe. Mum was a working-class woman, earning enough to maintain a sustainable living. We didn't need for much; Mum's love was more than we could ever ask for.

After building a solid and faith-filled relationship with our catholic priest, Mum often dropped me off to his home. He portrayed himself as a good canonical parson, someone I and others belonging to the church could confide in and trust. He showed absolutely no signs he was a child sex predator.

The first few times Mum took me to his home he came rushing to our aid, shaking Mum's hand, acknowledging my name, and greeting us both with a smile. He'd then provide Mum with assurance that I was in good hands and he would look after me, teaching me positive things about God and the work God does for his believers.

The priest also mentioned how excited he was to have me as his assistant. He said I wasn't just suitable, but a child who was able to carry out responsibilities belonging to the role of an altar boy with wisdom beyond my years. At that moment Mum felt proud, she felt good about her decision and that leaving me in his care would prepare me for the best of things to come. I don't remember not wanting to be there. I didn't have a father to hang out with, and the priest seemed a good substitute for the real thing. It was also an escape from my annoying siblings, even though I loved them.

On the first few occasions whilst in the company of the priest in his home I learnt about God, and what it meant to believe in him. The priest offered food and drink, with the casual sweet treats if I wanted. I remember him saying, "God looks after those that listen." At six years of age, I think I was pretty good at listening. I hardly ever disobeyed Mum, after all, she was the only adult role model left in my life after Dad walked out on us.

After the priest got to know me a little better and I felt comfortable learning about him, well, learning about the work of God, he invited me to stay over for the night. He said when my mum arrived to pick me up he'd ask her if it was okay for me to stay over some time. I didn't think anything of it, besides the fun I was having.

And then that day came, when Mum allowed the priest to look after me for a night. He reassured her I was in good hands and everything would be alright. After they agreed on a time for her to pick me up the following day, Mum gave me a big hug before getting back in her car and leaving. Reversing out of the driveway, she waved and shouted, "I love you," with a smile. I waved back and said, "I love you too." Although I was feeling something wasn't quite right, I simply ignored those feelings and followed the priest inside.

We went about our usual business, talking about God and all the good things God does for his believers. The priest laid out some food, supplied drinks, and again offered the casual sweet treat. After my time of learning about God was over, I got to play around on the piano or run amuck outside kicking a ball around, simply amusing myself to pass time.

That night the priest prepared a bed for me in the living room. He said I could watch TV and fall asleep. Who was I to disagree? What kid doesn't like to watch TV in the lounge with a few delicious snacks, watching a favourite movie? The only thing missing was my younger siblings.

A little while later I took a shower, got into my pyjamas, brushed my teeth and settled in for the night. Moments later, the priest put a movie on.

It wasn't a child's movie.

To my shock and horror, it was an adult movie. As mortified as I was, he began to tell me I'd enjoy watching it but wasn't to tell anyone.

He then laid down beside me and made himself comfortable, as if to suggest he too was settling in for a night of watching movies. What seemed only a few short moments later, he placed my hands on his genitals as he watched the adult movie. I remember feeling scared, petrified. My heart began to beat fast. I felt an overwhelming sudden onset of paralysis take over my entire body.

I was experiencing a feeling of sensory loss. I had lost the ability to move or say anything, and there he was getting an erection over my being beside him whilst watching an adult movie. He then grabbed my head and told me to taste his lollipop. In other words—to suck on his penis. He said he enjoyed getting his lollipop sucked on and that he would suck mine so I could feel the same kind of joy he did.

I didn't want to suck his lollipop/penis. I didn't even want to be there anymore. But what was a six-year-old to do? He forced my head into his lap after he had pulled his penis out from his underpants and told me to open my mouth, and that God does great things for those who listen.

I kept my mouth closed for quite a while, at least until he forced his fingers into my mouth and left me with absolutely no choice. I was in a position I never wanted to be in, encountering sexual abuse by a man who claimed to be of the righteousness of God.

The priest started touching me all over my body. He began running his lips and tongue around places that made me feel numb to the entire happening. I remember curling up and shutting my legs real tight with my bum cheeks clinched. I felt sick inside my stomach, scared, alone and defenceless. I lost my childhood and my innocence that night. I knew I'd never be the same young boy ever again.

The entire ordeal of being forced to do things I never wanted to felt like it had gone on for hours, even though, and I hate to say it, it lasted minutes, I think?

Afterwards, the priest said if I told anyone he would punish me, and God would punish me and my mum too.

The next day, a little after lunch from what I remember, Mum finally arrived to pick me up. I pretended I was okay, when deep down inside I wasn't. I learnt to become my very own award-winning actor. I felt too scared to mention anything to Mum for fear of God punishing me and her, and for fear the priest would punish me as well. I feared being rejected by the people I loved the most, and the people who loved me the most.

I was also scared what my school friends would say if they found out, and how they'd treat me. I made a conscious decision not to speak openly about my personal experience, even though it went on for a while after that one night. Somehow, within my subconscious I was able to disguise the shame I was feeling by hiding it and masking my reality in the cover-up of normality. As an adult looking back on that dreadful situation, I have often wondered how I was able to mask my emotions.

I have struggled with various emotions throughout my adult years, and in my marriage with two children and a stepchild. I would not allow my children to be cared for by other people, no matter how closely related they were. I often found myself secretly worried about what might happen to them. I didn't want my children to suffer the same way I did, having their childhood removed by someone I'd placed my trust in.

My wife learned about my childhood story during the earliest months of our first year in our relationship. I felt it was the right thing to do, although more importantly, it would explain my emotional outrage and emotional detachment from time to time. Admittedly those sorts of moments not only startled my wife, who was my girlfriend at the time, but many ended with her in tears, thinking she had done something wrong when she hadn't.

I felt my heart break every time my emotional outrage and detachment upset her. I didn't mean to cause her heartache, honestly. I just couldn't seem to control the feelings I was experiencing inside. Fortunately, my wife is an understanding woman who has more patience and empathy than anyone I've ever known. She is also very forgiving, although I think she knew something had happened to me well before I told her my childhood story, she just couldn't make out what exactly it was that was causing my emotional grief.

As time went by, my wife encouraged me to share my childhood abuse story with my mum and stepdad too. I didn't want to at first, but the more I deliberated over the thought of expressing my childhood experiences, the more I realised the emotional relief it was bound to provide me. Building up the courage took some time, but I got there in the end, and finally told my story to my mum and stepdad. My stepdad has always been there for me, as have my mum and my siblings.

On the day I expressed myself fully and completely the room was filled with silence, leading Mum to break down into emotional disarray. I felt severely debilitated by her upset. I love my mum, she was all I had as a child and all I wanted was for her to be happy, especially after my father left us high and dry.

My stepdad was speechless. He didn't know how to respond, but he was there for me, as he was for my mum. He hugged me, and eventually said, "The past is history and how we deal with it is up to us. You've done an amazing job to cover up such a terrible childhood tragedy. You hid your suffering well, and if you didn't open up to us like this we never would've guessed that you had experienced childhood trauma to this degree, nor would we have known you'd been suffering in silence all this time. We love you and we will always stand by you."

My telling of childhood experiences ended in a group hug, followed by individual hugs, along with many apologies, sighs of regret, sadness and a touch of anger. The room was filled with muddled emotions and no one could control what we were all individually experiencing.

In hindsight, disclosing my personal experiences of child molestation at any time during my life certainly wasn't easy, I still struggle with it today. But I knew deep down I had to talk about these things because of the recurring flashbacks, especially during mine and my wife's most physical and intimate moments. I couldn't cope with my reality emotionally or mentally anymore, even though I tried to suppress memories and continue with my life as if nothing ever happened. When lying about my emotions stopped working, I knew I needed to try another avenue to help break free and release my burdens.

Truth is, I have questioned my sexuality many times, often wondering if I might be gay, mostly because of my childhood experience of being sexually abused by that man. I have questioned myself, my thoughts and feelings, trying to decipher through mixed emotions of what is real and what isn't.

I remember erupting in anger, hate, and shame, telling my wife I didn't know who I was and that I wasn't sure if I was straight or gay.

I started to question my life choices, wondering if I only married her to protect myself from the shame of my past childhood life. My wife, however, was encouraging, and still is to this day. She seems to understand my battles, struggles and anguish with my past, and knows when to listen and to encourage me to talk more about these things. Without her love, support and encouragement I don't know who or what I might've been. It hasn't been easy, but like my wife often says, "Easy doesn't often transpire to beauty."

Many times, I have asked myself some really tough questions, and that has helped bring my truth to the surface. I sincerely hope my story and the following questions help others who have suffered.

Questions

Q: Did I at any time enjoy being sexually violated by the priest?
A: I certainly did not.

Q: Do I find men sexually attractive?
A: I'd be lying if I didn't say I find some men aesthetically attractive. Some men have great genetics and have worked hard at producing great muscle tone and fit bodies, but that doesn't mean I find myself sexually attracted to the male gender.

Q: Why would I think I'm gay if I didn't enjoy being sexually violated by that man?
A: It was my first sexual encounter and first ongoing sexual encounter, despite the amount of shame involved in saying that. The experience confused and demented my thinking.

Q: Should the first sexual encounter determine your sexuality for the rest of your life, regardless of how it made you feel?
A: No, it should not. If you're not born homosexual, you are heterosexual. We are all entitled to choice.

I'm in my mid-forties now, and I've gone from regular counselling to almost no counselling at all. My anger has largely dissipated, even though I still harbour feelings of shame.

The way I try to look at things now, and over the past years since meeting my wife and having children, is if I can give to my children what was taken away from me I am doing something right. To love, nurture and protect all three of my children is what I live for. I want my children to have what I didn't have—to remain untouched and pure.

They never got to experience sleepovers in their youngest years, as controlling and out of line as that may sound. My children are aware of what happened to me as a small boy. They needed to know so they could learn to understand and appreciate my reasons for making such decisions. My children's safety, health and wellbeing are my priority.

I am fortunate to have a wife who is far from vindictive, unrelenting or narcissistic. She is constant in genuine sincerity for me and my wellbeing, even during times when I've had complete meltdowns, and there have been many.

I'm so grateful for her love, compassion, genuine care and sincerity. And I'm especially fortunate to have three of the best children I could've ever asked for, even though in times of upset they'll throw some criticism toward me. I've learnt to laugh and shake it off.

When my reality sets in, I can deeply say I didn't enjoy being sexually abused by that man. I was a child, an innocent child. Even at six years of age I knew what he was doing to me wasn't right - it was wrong. It didn't feel good, it didn't feel right, and I hated it. For a long time I hated myself, and I hated him. For most of my life I've tried very hard not to allow this perpetrator to infect my biological thinking. So when I reflect over my deepest thoughts over the years that have gone by, I got married and had kids because I wanted a family and I believe it's what a heterosexual person is supposed to do. I ought to mention I've no discrimination or hate toward homosexuals. We all have our opinions and we all have a choice, and I've clearly made mine.

Opening up and coming clean about my childhood experience has allowed my inner being to lighten. I feel a huge, excessive weight has lifted from my shoulders. I saw dark clouds disappear and suddenly the sky was blue. Coming out as an abuse survivor felt ever more rewarding. I met with some powerful emotions that have changed my life, my feelings and my thinking, and it's forever.

I love my life, my wife and my children. I love my mum, my siblings and my stepdad too. They've all been super supportive and understanding through my most difficult and trying times and I thank them deeply and sincerely for that.

In our reality, there will always be challenges and great difficulties in the pursuit of our own happiness. I have had to push myself to think differently, to extend my comfort zones to silence disruptive noise in order to find peace.

Thanks to time and experience, I can now anticipate potential emotional problems. Forewarned is forearmed. When I feel an emotional change that heavily reflects on things relating to my childhood (emotional triggers) I find going for a long walk, talking to my mum, my stepdad, or speaking with my wife (and sometimes my children) most certainly helps, aside from a good night's sleep.

Learning to live with my damaging reality wasn't easy for me. It wouldn't be easy for anyone. Life doesn't become easy by chance. It simply gets better with change.

I've been changing the way I think since the age of six, trying to teach and coach myself to not let my past affect me in detrimental ways that could destroy my life and the people around me.

I've learnt a thing or two about living a positive life, and I'm still learning. Whilst I may sometimes struggle to let go of the past, I try very hard to look at my past as a temporary setback rather than a permanent one, even though it has somewhat permanently damaged my being. Rather than allowing it to manifest into permanent wreckage, I tend to also look at my emotions as a temporary setback, and I always find a way to build a bridge and get over it.

One of my greatest achievements in life is accepting myself before anyone else could, aside from my wife of course. Sharing my truth wasn't easy, but doing so liberated me. Genuine self-acceptance is accepting yourself irrespective of outcomes. I have accepted my fear of failure, I have accepted my fear in sharing my story with loved ones, and I have accepted my fear in sharing this story with you.

I cannot promise anyone who has been through a similar thing will live abundantly in positivity. They do, however, owe it to themselves to try.

I sincerely hope my story will help someone, if not save them from the deceit of similar evil.

Psalm 23:4

Even when I walk through the darkest valley, I will not be afraid, for you are close beside me. Your rod and your staff protect and comfort me.

Rising

We are known to sabotage our own lives when things are going well. It is simply a way of expressing our fear about whether we deserve to have a better life. Thought-provoking memories can cause obstructive thought processes, making us feel worthless and good-for-nothing. The challenge is not to be fearless, but to develop strategies that help to acknowledge our fears and find a way to palliate them.

In many cases, we are not able to control what happens to us, but we can control our reactions. We can choose to stay down for the count and be carried out of the ring, or we can pull ourselves back to our feet.

A wise person once said a bird does not worry that the branch it is perched on will break, because it puts its faith in its wings, not the branch. The same faith can be applied to ourselves.

Finding reason is finding the ability to rise above problems we face. That is our gift to ourselves.

- Changing our thought processes changes our reality. Choose thought processes wisely.

If you're going to look back on something that has hindered you, take from it what you know and turn it into beauty.

- Anger is a bad counsellor. Choose to be happy.
- What is beauty if it has no complex web? The emergence of complexity is beautiful and gratifying.
- Embrace vulnerability, let it be your greatest strength.
- Encouraging deliberate behavioural activation has its rewards.
- Give no accommodation to wreckage, give accommodation to refuge.

2
Marriage Annulment

(Joe, age 40)

We met as teenagers, a short time after I'd completed grade ten at high school. After leaving school, I commenced an apprenticeship in carpentry.

Late one Saturday afternoon, my friends and I decided to have a few drinks before heading out to a party, not too far from my parents' home. One of my best friends at the time was going out with a girl he'd invited around. She was accompanied by one of her friends, who she introduced to me. I wasn't one for having girlfriends. I wasn't all that experienced, was quite shy, and hadn't come out of my shell yet.

After a few drinks we started chatting. We got along, and at the end of the night we exchanged numbers. We kept in contact over the weeks and ended up arranging a meet up. From then on we became an item, agreeing to become a couple (boyfriend and girlfriend).

My girlfriend worked a part-time job in retail for a few years before quitting to work part-time in aged care. I don't know what she did with the money she earned, but we managed to make do with what we had at the time. Five years later and out of my apprenticeship, I was able to save enough money from my job as a carpenter to place a deposit on our first home.

Six months after moving in, my girlfriend fell pregnant with our first child. It was unexpected, as we didn't plan to have children and had never discussed it. Financially we weren't in a position to have them, and ultimately, I hadn't intended a life with children. We had both been practicing safe sex and she claimed to have been on contraception. I spoke to her about having an abortion, but nothing came of it. A little later in her pregnancy, I felt our relationship started to change for the worse.

The position I found myself in with her created an extreme amount of unwanted pressure that caused me to feel stressed and anxious about the future. I felt an immense external pressure for the simple fact that we weren't exactly well-settled or financially prepared, and that put me on the back foot. I felt she had manipulated the situation, causing me to feel trapped.

I felt our relationship took a drastic emotional and physical downturn when the first child was born. I felt deceived by her, with no way out. Despite the outcome and given no choice in the matter, reflecting on it now, I realise I did the best I could as a loving and supportive partner and father.

As time went on, noticeable changes became more apparent, including lack of communication or physical attraction between the two of us. My girlfriend put on an excessive amount of weight after the birth of our first child and she struggled to lose it. She'd often complain about her size and how she didn't feel good about herself. She had access to my accounts to buy all the things she needed to help make herself feel good again, though sadly nothing she tried worked. Her efforts were deemed worthless with no results in weight change, and her complaints kept on coming.

Whilst I sometimes tried to empathise and support her, I often felt physically tired and emotionally drained, especially after a long day at work. I'd work up to ten hours most days, sometimes six days a week, and arriving home to an untidy house with stuff all over the place and no dinner on the table was disheartening. I felt unappreciated and taken advantage of. Matters grew worse, our sex life was almost non-existent and our intimate moments weren't particularly great.

Eighteen months later she became pregnant with our second child. Another unplanned pregnancy I wasn't prepared for, and again she knew that. I don't know how it was possible for her to fall pregnant, because she had specifically told me she was using prescribed contraception tablets. Basically, my girlfriend reiterated that she was on the pill, and as an additional precautionary measure to prevent more pregnancies, I'd used condoms, though sex for us wasn't all that often. Furthermore, I felt it necessary to wear condoms because she wasn't the most hygienic person. She had a bad vaginal odour and I struggled to cope with it, finding it difficult to get an erection. It's also something I never brought to her attention because I didn't know how to, and I didn't want to hurt her feelings, despite my own. We were quite the opposite when it came to hygiene and cleanliness, so much so I often questioned myself on what I saw in her.

Further into our relationship I started drinking regularly, often becoming intoxicated, yet somehow, and on the rarest of occasions, I managed to gain an erection long enough to get it up and put it in. Our sexual encounters would only last a minute or two and then I'd roll over and fall to sleep.

Despite my depressive state and ignoring my feelings, one and a half years later we ended up getting married. I felt it was the right thing to do for my children's sake. I guess when you come from a small family where your parents have been together most of their lives, despite what you see them put themselves through to satisfy marriage vowels you take on similar traits, almost leading you to become habitually lazy in spite of recognised emotions that you end up in battle with.

With the arrival of the second child, I renovated the house to make a little more room for additional comfort. A small house, it was all I could afford on my earnings. Renovations took up all my spare time and nearly all my hard-earned money. I started drinking a hell of a lot more, which then led to an excessive smoking habit, including marijuana. When that wasn't enough, I'd increase my marijuana intake. I was high every day, feeling sick and tired of my life. Bored with routine, I ended up dabbling in recreational drugs, although I couldn't afford it.

Four years later, and call me a fool because in all honesty I felt like one, the third unplanned child came along. I wasn't sure if this child was mine or not, and when she was born I felt she wasn't. She looked different from the other two, looking more like one of our mutual friends with blonde hair and blue eyes. Neither I nor my wife had these distinctive features and blue eyes don't exist in either of our families. Curiosity grew and I asked my wife if there was something she needed to tell me. She denied having other sexual relationships, despite spending a lot of time at our mutual friend's house. Because there was no factual evidence, I had no choice but to believe her. Despite my feelings, I love the child like she is mine and I don't treat her any differently, but I still ponder over particular happenings during that marriage. Some things don't make sense, and in reflection I felt lied to, manipulated and cheated.

Because the family unit was growing, the kids had to share rooms. By this stage I was spending most of my time in the shed out the back of the house, enjoying my own company every chance I had, while becoming silently more depressed with the burden of financial woes. I'd drink myself to sleep some nights, but with lots of bills to pay I somehow still found the energy and willpower to maintain my job. Nothing like a mortgage to get you out of bed every day! I ended up having to do cash jobs outside of my regular job just to pay bills. My life became consumed with work after that.

Three girls and eighteen months after the third child my wife became pregnant with the fourth child. This time it was planned, because I thought, "What the heck, what difference is a fourth child going to make?" Plus, I wanted a boy, someone I could potentially relate to. Though I got my wish, a little while down the track my son was diagnosed autistic. I'm not sure if that was the result of the alcohol and drug abuse, good chance, though scientifically not proven. My current girlfriend read in the Introduction to Psychology Sixth Edition by Rod Plotnik that in the 1950s, psychologists explained that children became autistic if they were reared by parents who were cold and rejecting (Blakeslee, 2000a). This could be true considering our relationship and feelings towards one another. When I reflect on the youngest two children, each suffers with cognitive deficiencies, the second youngest also suffers with anxiety and panic disorder. I've also noticed her mood swings are often quite extreme. While I've read that extreme mood changes could potentially be bipolar, no diagnosis has confirmed this. Again, cognitive deficiencies are likely to result from continuous alcohol and drug consumption, known as Fetal Alcohol Syndrome. I wasn't thinking about the overall effects of my explicit use of such things, but this is the consequence I now have to live with for the rest of my life.

After the arrival of the fourth child the house became way too small for six people, one of the reasons I ended up spending most of my time after work in the back shed. I needed my own space, so I created a man shed I could enjoy. There was a pool table, dartboard, a TV with Sony PlayStation, a beer fridge and homebrew. I made 180 full bottles of beer that sat on the shelves at any one time. My homebrew turned out to be a saviour for me. They were good tasting beers, although I sold more than I drank. All the work boys seemed to enjoy it, and even my dad was buying my homebrew beer. I think Dad was just trying to support me as he knew my financial strains, because he's by no means a heavy drinker, more of an occasional drinker if anything.

A little later down the track, my heart and spirit began feeling more burdened. I started indulging in my homebrew and drank a lot more bourbon. I put on fifteen kilograms over three years drinking homebrew. Lunch was often toasted sandwiches and dinner was often poor-quality food, because that's all she would make. Sometimes I'd have to fend for myself. Life with my wife had become deeply depressing and I wasn't in a good way spiritually, mentally or physically. I had contemplated suicide several times as an escape from my internal sufferings.

Nine years after I purchased that first property, I had to sell it to buy another one as we needed a larger abode to cater for all our growing needs. Once again, I spent all my spare time and what little money I had renovating the house with my dad.

My relationship became almost non-existent. Well, that's how I felt anyway. There was no love, no support or appreciation. We didn't do things together. Admittedly, I just didn't want to spend time with her, let alone be seen with her. Sadly, when my wife and the kids went to her friend's for a few hours I felt excited. I'd quietly celebrate, thinking *Woohoo, I have the freedom to do what I want to in the house I'm paying for!*

In hindsight, I spent all of the time and money I had trying to sustain a comfortable lifestyle fit for the entire family, whilst working my fingers to the bone for lousy pay and feeling emotionally stressed and physically depleted.

Things got extremely tight, because I was the one paying for everything. I felt tired, drained and exhausted, and coming home to a loveless relationship, a messy home and no dinner cooked on occasions made me feel used, sad, unwanted, depressed and unappreciated. As much as I enjoyed working, I didn't enjoy not having a single dollar to spend on myself. I also didn't enjoy arriving home to a loveless relationship, and what was even sadder, at the end of every week there was no money left in the account, she consumed every cent that was left after the mortgage and bills went out.

In 2010 I'd had enough. I needed to spend some of my own hard-earned money spoiling myself for once. So I went out and bought a brand new XR6 utility vehicle with chrome ladder racks, under tray tool boxes, tow bar, paint protection and tinted windows. I went all out. I'd finally spoilt myself after sixteen years of letting her spend all my money (aside from the bills and ongoing maintenance on the house).

Fast forward to mid-year 2012, I had the opportunity to do fly-in fly-out work. There was good money on offer with three weeks on/one week off so I jumped at the opportunity. At that stage of my relationship, and at that point in my life, work was a holiday for me. I couldn't have felt happier than to live away from the wife.

Six months into my new job, I was home on my rest and recovery week. The kids' mother needed to have a chat, so we sat down and talked it out. She said she wasn't happy and our marriage wasn't working out. I told her I wasn't happy and the feeling was mutual. I mentioned marriage counselling to help resolve our twenty years of marriage issues. Again, my parents are still married and even though they had problems in their relationship, they would work things out. When I reflect on this one thing about my parents and the values I had learned, I guess I was trying to do the same, even though I knew in my heart nothing was going to work and I had had enough.

Despite trying to offer a resolution, the kids' mother said we both had our own problems to deal with before we could think about doing anything as a couple, marriage counselling wouldn't help. She continued to say she had problems of her own to sort out and that I needed to seek professional help regarding my drinking problems and depression. As cowardly as I may seem, I was again just trying to do the right thing traditionally.

For a number of years I had contemplated suicide, mostly because I felt forced into a life I never wanted. Ironically, she was the cause of my illicit habits but couldn't see what she had created, being so self-absorbed. Everything had to be about her, nothing was ever about me. She wanted what she wanted and I foolishly gave it to her, believing every word she said. I foolishly allowed her to manipulate me into having children when she damn well knew my feelings.

Fortunately, the company I worked for at the time had a counselling program that supported these types of issues. After four sessions of getting everything off my chest to a stranger I felt some form of relief. A little while later, and despite my feelings because I was thinking of the children, I raised the issue again with the wife to try and save the marriage. But nothing ever came of it and we ended up parting ways. When I look back on this now, it was the best thing to happen to me. Separating did me the world of good and led to our divorce. To my relief, a huge weight was finally released and I could feel somewhat normal again.

Within twelve months the divorce papers were signed, sealed, and delivered. The house then went on the market and sold quickly, leaving me with a small profit. I paid the ex-wife half of what I received and deposited fifty thousand dollars into her bank account. She also got to keep the family wagon and all the household furnishings. I was finally free.

Whilst we gladly went our separate ways, I felt undeniably sad. But I also knew it was the best thing to happen over and above all else. At that stage I was living with my parents, trying to recover from financial losses. With what money I had left after the divorce settlement I began to work on myself in any way I could.

I continued to work in FIFO, earning enough money to put some away and to cover child support payments of $800 per week through a private agreement. Admittedly it wasn't really a private agreement because the ex-wife went on the single parent pension with Centrelink (a government support service that delivers social security payments and services to all Australians.) I've learnt that anything attached to government handouts requires full-time working-class individuals like me to pay a lot more. Well, that's what I believe. Though what I believe and what Child Support believes are two different things!

The ex-wife wasn't one to work full-time, despite the ability to. I guess she grew accustomed to living life getting what she wanted with little to no effort. Sadly, she saw me as her cash machine for many years, and I let her. Now she's doing the same to the government, taking advantage of government handouts despite having the physical and mental ability to work. She has also claimed the solo parent pension whilst in relationships with different men who lived under the same roof as her. While it's none of my business, it is after all tax payers' money that is going to her. But that's who she is, and I recognise this now.

Working away from home and getting divorced was what saved me emotionally. I also made a few good friends on the worksite who were supportive and understanding. They are still good friends to this day.

After straightening out my life, and with the love and support of my parents, I was able to save enough money to purchase another house. I lived alone in the new house for approximately five months, during which time I met an independent and beautiful woman who is now my girlfriend.

This woman is the antithesis of the previous one. She has enhanced my life in ways I never could've imagined. She has two adult children in their early twenties, so with my four we have six children combined.

Getting to know my girlfriend, including her past (which is relatively sad), I have learnt how compatible we are. When I think of her, I realise how understanding, smart, talented, artistic, creative and streetwise she is. She's taught me the foundation of true partnership and helped me to get ahead, turning debts into assets whilst living within financial means and appreciating every dollar we both earn. She explains things to me in a way no one else has, pulls me up on things that aren't quite right and is very much an ideas type of woman. And she's a go getter with a loving nature. For the most part we are strongly compatible, with the same outlook on life.

I'm so fortunate to come home to a woman who can cook, is house proud, has flair, looks after herself and is hygienically clean. And even though she works, she manages to have this fine-tuned balance of all things. She's been through a lot in her life and she's done a lot too, more than I ever have.

My girlfriend has helped to change my overall outlook on life and I thank her so much for that. I've gone from heavy drinking to just enjoying an occasional drink, I no longer smoke marijuana and I've almost given up cigarette smoking. I am more motivated and energised, and I enjoy my girlfriend's company more than anything. That's a big change from a twenty-year marriage with a woman who was self-absorbed, manipulating, lazy, grubby and co-dependent.

I don't ever want to go back to where I once was. I am at my happiest now, more than ever. My life overall has dramatically improved, and every year it just seems to get better and better, especially on a physical, mental and emotional level.

Declaration

Casting back on the story of Marriage Annulment, helping and giving is part of the human characteristic, although the reverse effect is the immense amount of self-sacrifice humans often make. Sometimes helpful intentions can create acquiesce, causing capitulating dysfunctional behaviours that grow in each of us. We don't need to cease all giving to prevent human behaviours like this, but we do need to create boundaries to help minimise co-dependency, irresponsible incompetence and poor character.

There are times we all need to face the fact that our good intention of giving has gone bad. Continuing to give under such circumstances is a huge waste of time, energy and resources that also runs the risk of potential health issues. That leads to an increased risk of developing mental health problems, followed by the depletion of spiritual energy that then transcends into sad emotions which can quickly spiral into depression.

There are significant differences between healthy and unhealthy giving behaviours. Healthy giving promotes growth, independence and positivity, while unhealthy dysfunctional giving promotes the opposite. When the diametrical opposite happens, the other person has violated agreements. When we choose to continually give to people who don't uphold agreements and have betrayed our trust, anger and resentment kicks in. It is at that point we need to stop providing them with chances. Also, dependent on the person involved or the situation you are dealing with, you may want to wait until they can provide strong evidence they are ready to fulfil their end of the agreement and progress in life.

When you have a distinct feeling, or have been given a distinct impression, you're being manipulated into believing stories to persuade you into helping or giving. For example, when someone says things to trigger guilt, then conveniently provides you with a giving opportunity that will reduce your guilt, you are being manipulated. This is a sign they are willing to deceive and take advantage of you to get what they want, without giving you what you want.

Manipulation is a sign of someone who is willing to be deceitful, taking advantage of other people's good nature in a skilful, unscrupulous manner, and often at any expense. Manipulating personalities have selfish motives and will dominate the other using guilt trip methods to win favour for themselves.

Healthy giving goes without sacrificing your physical or mental wellbeing, your self-worth or your financial security. If you feel you are being lied to, manipulated or taken advantage of, back out of giving immediately. If you don't, the risk of going ahead could sap everything you've worked long and hard for; whether internal or external, both are equally important.

If you are in a fraught, imbalanced relationship where there is conflict, one-sided control, hurt and resentment, if you are feeling manipulated or emotionally abused, whether male or female, these behaviours should never be acceptable. Emotional abuse and manipulation are emotional blackmail. It is unfair behaviour and you need to eliminate it quickly.

Key points to Help You Deal with a Manipulating Partner or Spouse:

- Do not brush their behaviours under the rug or treat them as if they are no big deal. Bring their behaviours to their attention by calling them out on it. The point is, say no to being manipulated and put an end to it right away. Treating their manipulating habits as if they don't exist will cause you harm in the long run.

- If manipulation in your relationships continues, set boundaries or seek marriage counselling. Do not try to correct manipulating personalities, because correcting them won't work. Remember, manipulating personalities aim to sink you deeper into their trap, so you must find a way to hit their centre of gravity. In some cases, you may not know what their centre of gravity is and it might take you a little while to discover it. Once you find out what that centre of gravity is, make it yours.
- Trust your judgement. Only you know what's truly best for your life. Don't follow customary ways that you've learnt from others, because they are not likely to work for you. Remember—parents, friends and relatives grew up in different times. What worked for them may not work for you. We are all different, and what works for one person may not work for another, it's a case-by-case basis. Times are also changing, and the decisions we need to make must fit within those times.
- Stop looking to other people to define who you are or what you want to do with your life. Define yourself. One of the greatest things that separates you from other people is not the ability to always listen to other people's beliefs—it's the ability to listen to *your own* beliefs. Beliefs are your boundaries. They are often self-created values that give your life meaning. By setting boundaries and holding strong to your self-created values you will prevent manipulating people from affecting your life.
- Don't try to fit in. Continue to reinvent your life and make the best of it. Manipulating people rely on consistent

behaviours so they can count on you to push their agendas forward. They want you to show up every day with your hand full so they can take from you what you won't give to yourself. Consistency is how manipulators keep you in lockdown. It's how they control you.

- Cease compromising with manipulators. Guilt is a useless emotion, though it's generally a powerful tool. Guilt is one of the most common weapons manipulators will use against you. They will make you feel guilty if you choose to decide against an agenda that has come to light. For example, unplanned pregnancies are a common one. Couples who have spoken about their futures together will often discuss children. Not all couples want to have children, at least until they know they are financially secure and are prepared to make life changes that create happier times for all involved. When contraception has been discussed and both parties are practicing safe sex pregnancy is unlikely. When a manipulating personality is involved the chance of pregnancy heightens through the use of a hidden agenda. The manipulator will stoop to the level of deception that will provide them the results they want, no matter the cost and in spite of the other person's feelings or visons for the future.
- Manipulators are good at being vague. Pretending not to have details, or hiding what they know to be truthful, is their way of avoiding in-depth discussions that would reveal truth. Manipulators are often far from truthful.
- Stop being a sucker. Work on an exit plan, know your purpose in life and take responsibility for yourself. Stop being a punching bag or a doormat and letting manipulating

personalities walk all over you. Have enough self-awareness and self-respect to say no to people who treat you poorly.

- Unfortunately, manipulating people do exist. Yes, their actions are wrong, but that doesn't mean you get a free pass to make mistakes and be walked all over. No one can manipulate you without your permission, even if you've become numb to it all. You are responsible for your own mistakes in life, just as much as your successes. Be accountable and learn from your mistakes.
- Don't trust the same slippery person over and over again. Cut them loose, delete them from your life, and try to do that early in the relationship, otherwise you'll have to endure long-term costly consequences, whether you like it or not.

Manipulation is a Form of Emotional Abuse

When emotional abuse is ongoing, a victim may lose their entire sense of self and self-worth, sometimes without a single scar or bruise. Victims will hide their emotional wounds, making them invisible to others, hidden in self-doubt, worthlessness and self-loathing.

In some cases, emotional abuse can be so severe that it erodes the victim's sense of self so much that they no longer see themselves realistically. Consequently, the victim then agrees with the abuser, becoming numb to all that surrounds them. Once this happens, most victims become trapped, with long-lasting or permanent repercussions.

Repercussions

Every single action and decision we make comes with consequences, whether we are conscious of it or not.

- Conscious choices are made with the information at hand, the risks understood and the implications of the risks known.
- Too often people lack courage. Instead of deciding what to do, having understood potential risks on a conscious level, the decision is made to defer a decision.
- Decisions without consciousness have a flip side of unwelcome repercussions. It is important to think through one's course of action before acting.
- Consciousness requires careful deliberation.
- Decisions without consciousness can lead to a lifetime of regret.
- It is best to make our way through life as purposefully as possible.
- To think before you act is to prevent unwanted consequences.
- Acting before thinking is called impulsivity and is detrimental to you making correct decisions and successful actions.
- Failing to think before you act can harm you, and those around you, in more ways than one.
- We should constantly review our actions to avoid having to apologise for our transgressions.
- Leaving transgressions unfixed and unowned is where the real abuse and damage takes place.
- The adage 'Hastes make waste' is especially true when it is exhibited by our words or actions that take place without careful consideration of thoughts.
- Stepping in front of a moving train is a really bad idea. Much of life is like that, literally or figuratively.
- To consider consequences of possible actions, and to consider alternative courses of possible actions, are hallmark traits of a good thinker.

Personal Transformation

- You cannot always control external people and events that happen in life. The secret is that everything changes when you change yourself.
- The greatest gifts known to mankind are life and the power of choice.
- Is there something in your life that needs changing? You have everything you need right now to change it.
- We have the power within ourselves to transform our own life.
- To get what you want out of life you must first know what the outcome, your desired end result, looks like.
- When was the last time you sat down and defined your current problems and visualised what resolution and transformation would look like? Don't just think about it. Make your resolution concrete and write it down.

Write a list of things you need to change and list the reasons why you need to change them.

- Write down all the wonderful things that will result from change and transformation. This will give you something to reflect on when you start to lose motivation or temptation tries to revert you back into your same old habits.

Remember that change is a gradual process, and most big changes are made by taking small steps everyday over a long period of time.

- Sometimes in life, all it takes is a stranger.
- Personal transformation takes time. It is not something that simply happens overnight and it's not linear. Sometimes you

will take three steps forward then two steps back. Other times you'll make leaps and bounds.

- Change always involves learning, and constant learning defines life.
- We can all learn from mistakes. Emotional scar tissue makes us infinitely more resilient.
- It's good to learn from the journeys and mistakes of others. Often, they've already experienced a similar journey to the one you're embarking upon, cutting your learning experience in half.

Restoration

Don't beat yourself up. Negative self-talk can be a slippery slope that continues to adversely affect your life. Consider what you need to let go of to heal and forgive yourself.

- There is restorative justice in deciding or agreeing to walk away from anything that prohibits wellbeing and happiness.

Ending a toxic relationship and accepting that it's time to move on can be difficult. It can also be hard to shake off everything you went through. You may end up thinking of yourself as a victim and pity yourself.

- You're allowed to feel angry and have mixed emotions about everything you endured, including the end of that relationship, but you need to recognise which emotions are serving you and which ones are keeping you from moving forward.
- Give your emotional wounds time to heal. Don't rush yourself through the process, be patient so you can learn to appreciate what that relationship taught you.

- The only reason you should be thinking about your toxic relationship is to grow from it, not to fixate on it.
- You can't change people or the past. It happened, you learned, and it's time to move on.
- How blessed it is to stumble upon a soul who wants nothing but the best for you for the rest of your life.
- Divine healing is not just for one part of a person. It's not just for the spirit, thy emotions, thy soul or thy body. It's for every part of the human anatomy.
- The mind, the will and the emotions make up the personality of a human being.

The mind affects our emotions. We must discipline and renew our minds because that is the battlefield. Thoughts bear fruit, and thoughts bring results. If you think it long enough, you'll believe it. If you think it long enough, you'll do it.

- At one time or another in life we have all experienced wounds, disappointments, failed relationships, physical pain, financial troubles and so much more. Deep wounds require deep healing.
- To experience spiritual and emotional freedom from a painful past we must understand the link between spiritual warfare and inner healing.
- Sometimes struggles are what we need. They make us stronger than we often choose to realise.
- The art of healing is within the capacity of everyone.
- Be true to yourself and don't stay in a miserable marriage for the sake of providing your children a stable home. You need love in your life too.

- Emotional healing is not so much about getting better. It's about letting go of everything that isn't you.
- Talking to a stranger may be challenging and intimidating, but you will likely feel much better afterward and be able to move to better and bigger things.
- While it's essential to share and express what's happened to you, it's also equally important to take care of yourself while you're moving forward with your life.
- Self-compassion and forgiveness are just as important as the processing of the breakup.
- Letting go of someone is hard, however, healing begins with bravely acknowledging what you've been through.
- Processing a toxic, unhealthy relationship will not always be graceful, but you can train yourself to focus on the positive by finding creative ways to spend your time.
- When the uncertain road to recovery overwhelms you and it feels almost impossible to keep going, remind yourself of this: Ultimately, I have control over what I want for my life, even when it feels impossible to envision the future.
- Give yourself permission to enjoy single life for a bit. Use the time to recharge your energy levels.
- Keep yourself looking forward by creating achievable goals.
- Achievable goals keep you motivated and allow you the time to prepare physically, emotionally, spiritually, and financially.

3
Swallowed Wreckage

(Anna, age 55)

I wouldn't be alive today if it weren't for my oldest son calling in at my home for a visit.

How did I get there? My childhood was happy and joyful, even though I was diagnosed with Attention Deficit Disorder (ADD). I had loving and supportive parents who were always there for me, through thick and thin.

Mum and Dad were remarkable people who set the bar quite high. Dad was my comfort and Mum was the working-class example. They were the entrepreneurial couple who had it together early in their marriage. Mum could only give birth to one child, me, so a little while later they legally adopted four more. Our family was then made up of myself, one other sister and three brothers.

Mum was often busy juggling many things, from cooking lovely meals to building rock walls, making fences, gardening, knitting small clothes, sewing clothes, designing a new home, all whilst nurturing all our animals and looking after all us kids. Mum always had some kind of plan, her head filled with many ideas, complete with vision. She was constantly on a mission, creating ways to provide a better lifestyle for our family and our future.

Mum was kind, but quite stern, especially when giving orders or disciplining us kids, Dad included. She was always the one to lay down the rules or punish us for disobedience, while Dad would pretend to. There was no arguing with her or trying to influence her in ways that we'd all be satisfied with, it was her way or the highway.

Dad was the easy-going one. He became a 'yes' man and said yes to almost everything. I guess it was the easiest way to settle things without the headache, so Mum always got her way.

My first marriage wasn't what I expected because my childhood was good, and even though I had my concerns, I loved him and married him anyway. There were obvious cultural differences, which brought along different viewpoints but also made our relationship interesting.

It took me a while to get used to my husband telling me what to do. He'd set out many daily tasks, besides the daily household duties. My husband was controlling, and I allowed him to control me. For the most part, I have a soft, sentimental heart, and like my Dad became a 'yes' woman and simply did what I was told. When my husband asked me to do something and I didn't do it straight away, he'd burst into a fit of rage. He'd anger so easily, causing me to feel fearful for my safety, even though he never actually laid a hand on me.

My husband put many holes in the walls of our home, at every outrageous episode. The house we had purchased together went from a homely abode to a wreckage real fast. I struggled to maintain upkeep, mostly because of the way it looked. Looking at holes in the walls every day was extremely demotivating and made me feel sad.

Despite my abusive husband who struggled to manager his anger, I cannot deny the sexual chemistry. Together we had five beautiful children.

During our life together, I'm sad to say, each of those children witnessed their father's angry rampages. It hurts me to admit and say that every day our children lived in fear. When my husband arrived home from work the children wouldn't make a sound for fear of upsetting him. They'd line themselves up on the couch in front of the TV, quietly hoping their father wouldn't punish them for nothing. As a mother, it was hard to witness. I grew to dislike my husband, grew a voice, and eventually left him.

My oldest son suffered the most throughout my marriage to his father. My husband was extremely hard on him, often beating him with physical, emotional and mental torment. And I let him. I tried hard to stand in his way, however he was far stronger than me. I've never been one for confrontation, and as much as I feared for my children's safety and wellbeing, I also feared for our lives.

Looking back on my marriage, it was an extremely controlling relationship where I ended up losing my internal happiness whilst slowly slipping into a depressive state of confusion. I was happy to leave my husband after eighteen years of marriage, for all that it was worth. I grew very tired of his abusive and eruptive ways. Enough was enough, so I walked away. The relationship remains amicable today.

I maintain close relationships with all my children. Despite the poor choices I've made, they have never stopped loving me. I will never stop loving them till the day I die.

Post-divorce, I placed my first marriage behind me and soon met another man who turned out to be no better than the first one. An alcoholic and a womaniser, he often broke up with me so he could pursue other women. After his relationships with them (there were many) he'd come back to me. The awful thing was I'd gladly take him back. I suppose I was hopeful, thinking he'd learn to love me, and love me unconditionally.

In the back of my mind, I was hoping our relationship would improve and that all things would get better. Then one day he left me yet again to pursue another woman. On a deep and emotional level, I couldn't cope anymore. I had been prescribed antidepressants and decided to take a handful of them with the intent of falling to sleep—indefinitely.

Ten minutes after I took the antidepressants, my eldest son unexpectedly walked into my room. He had called around for a quick visit. I took one look at him and realised I couldn't do it; it would be selfish of me to leave my kids behind. I told my son what I'd just done and he rushed me to the nearest hospital, driving like a madman in fear of losing his mother.

By the time we arrived at the hospital I was feeling legless and incoherent. I had kept the medicine bottle with me. I don't remember much after that. In and out of consciousness, I remember waking up and seeing members of my family who'd come to visit me at the hospital.

The hospital instructed suicide risk. I couldn't leave until I had regular meetings set up with an appointed psychologist. A few days after the incident, my boyfriend decided to get back with me. I guess he felt bad that I'd tried to commit suicide over him.

A little while after that episode I decided to leave him. He started crying like a baby, dropped to his knees and proposed to me! Silly me said yes, even though he had hurt me repeatedly. There was no denying I was heavily in love with the man.

Six months after we married, we moved from New Zealand to start a brand-new life in Cobar, Australia. Despite the promise of positive changes, atmosphere and surroundings, my husband continued to repeat his womanising ways. Relationship matters worsened when he started taking things out on my youngest daughter. He would lay down the law with her, acting as if he were her real father, questioning where she had been, what she'd been up to, and who with. He became physically abusive towards her too. I remember he purposely slammed her leg in the car door because she wouldn't get out of the car fast enough.

My husband would snap very quickly. I often wondered if he had bipolar, but to this day there has been no diagnosis for his erratic mood changes. Our relationship didn't last long. He returned to New Zealand to be closer to his family, during which time we tried to work through our differences but failed to rise above our issues. I am still married to my husband because getting a divorce is awfully difficult. Truth is, he ended up in prison on manslaughter charges for killing his sister.

Despite knowing the difficulty, heartbreak and suffering inside, I continue to live my life the way I want. I met another man who seems to care about me. He has helped me to see that not all men are abusive or violent. He does talk about his ex-wife a lot, and other girlfriends he's had, and he likes to drink beer, downing a few cans of XXXX Gold most nights. He has admitted he's an alcoholic, but I don't judge him on that. I'm just happy there's a man in my life who loves me, and I feel satisfied.

We accept the love we think we deserve.

Stephen Chbosky

https://www.goodreads.com/quotes/2534-we-accept-the-love-we-think-we-deserve

≈

Searching for love in all the wrong places
with all the wrong partners is analogous
to an addict craving drugs.

Insight and Reflections

When it comes to those we love and care about, it can be a right struggle to sit back and not want to involve yourself in the decisions they make, especially when they've had a history of repeated relationship mistakes.

What possesses people to choose the wrong partners time and time again? Let's break this story down so we can better understand the potential cause and effect.

Both relationships had similar characteristics, with traits of wrath embedded in both men.

The woman's childhood was described as a good one, with both parents being entrepreneurial types, striving to make a difference with their kids and grandkids in mind. So how does someone who comes from quality raising with exemplary parents end up in abusive relationships that eventually turn tumultuous and conclude disastrously?

Let's take a closer look to uncover the answer. She unknowingly describes the answer to the above questions as follows:

> "My first marriage wasn't what I expected because my childhood was good, and even though I had my concerns, I loved him and married him anyway."

Is this a woman who loves to no end, or a woman who doesn't love herself?

We cannot be sure if this woman actually lived a quality childhood life as she describes. We can only make assumptions, leading to inaccurate or accurate presumptions of what could be appropriate.

Could it be that this woman doesn't love herself enough, and that she has suffered with low self-esteem all her life with little confidence within herself? If so—what are the possible root causes for her lack of confidence and emotional suffering?

Could it be that she had an unstable parental figure who may have criticized her throughout her childhood, leaving her with complexities she's never been able to overcome?

Or was it that each of her incoherent and wrathful marriages left her broken, tired and feeling rejected?

When a woman becomes accustomed to abuse, whether from childhood experience, a parental figure or relationships, it is very possible that she is choosing relationships that repeat the criticism, wounding, abandonment and rejection because of the familiarity with the primary individuals. In a sense, she is finding comfort in familiar scenarios, even if those familiar scenarios in her relationships are filled with perturbation.

The bigger problem with toxic relationship cycles is that the longer a person continues in this cycle, the more their sense of any self-worth they have left erodes. This then indicates the bigger battle people will have in removing themselves from the pleasure/pain pattern they are trapped in.

When you are ready to let go of suffering from low self-esteem, and ready to combat feelings of self-doubt, such as negative self-talk or the incessant need to compare yourself to others, you will see just how amazing you are and you'll be better equipped to attract the right people into your life.

> How do you learn to recognise the signs of unhealthy dynamics whilst constantly craving partners who are not emotionally, mentally and wholesomely available?

What do you think are the root causes of her suffering? Is it that she doesn't love herself enough and suffers from low self-esteem and little confidence?

Could it be that she has an unstable parental figure who criticized her throughout her childhood, leaving her with complexities that she's never been able to overcome? Or did her incoherent and wrathful marriages leave her broken, tired, and feeling rejected? What answers did you come up with, and why?

Write your thoughts here:

Your thoughts are your findings. How do your findings relate to a situation you may have experienced? Have your findings been able to shine some light on your own situation?

____

____

____

____

____

It is said that when we *know* our worth, we don't let chemistry cloud our own ability to know it. The moment we choose to accept less, we get less, and the moment we accept disrespect and disregard, we set the precedent.

4

Miracle Man

(John, age 35)

I was born in Ipswich, a western district of Brisbane, Australia, to an Indigenous woman who was a heroin addict. My birth wasn't meant to be, so soon after the birth my biological mother placed me up for adoption.

My adoptive parents had two daughters already and were on the waiting list for a son. I was a few weeks old according to paperwork that shows my date of birth and the details of my legal adoption.

Back in the 1970s there were three categories of babies - the perfect baby, disabled baby, and retarded baby. The adoption agency described me to my soon-to-be parents, and a little while later I was on my way home with them. In my adoptive family there's Mum, Dad, me and two older sisters, making me the youngest.

A small portion of my childhood was spent on Stradbroke Island, which lies within the Moreton Bay region and forms part of the Australian state of Queensland. We lived on Stradbroke Island for approximately four years before moving to the mainland. I remember Dad owned a speed boat and we travelled to the mainland regularly before it became too much and schooling became an important matter.

Dad was the only ambulance officer on the island at the time. He was gifted with many talents, and saving lives was one of them. When we moved to the mainland, Dad became the head ambulance officer for Capalaba, a suburb that forms part of the Redland City Council. Life for all of us became so much more enjoyable after our move and we settled in quickly.

At primary school I excelled in sports and was recognised age champion. I was good at all sports, although I loved footy mainly, and athletics too. When I reached high school things changed. My grades weren't that great, my math was really bad and my interest in athletics became almost null and void. My love for football, soccer, AFL and cooking kept me going and got me through the rest of my high school years. In my final year I started thinking about my future. Cooking seemed like a good option, so once school finished I got myself a job.

The job was a three-year vocational traineeship provided by a government-funded course provider. Upon completion, you'd end up working full-time with RPL (recognised prior learning). The RPL is then added to your curriculum and somewhat reduces the overall time spent towards learning and obtaining the full and final qualification. Ultimately, I wanted to be a chef. Sadly, I had a lot of self-doubt, mostly due to my grades, so I chose to do the kitchen attendant traineeship instead.

After completing course requirements and graduating with my certificate at the Princess Alexandra Hospital in Brisbane, I landed a kitchen hand position at the Story Bridge Hotel (one of Brisbane's most iconic pubs), located just across the river from Brisbane CBD. Built in 1886, the hotel was first known as the Kangaroo Point Hotel, until it was renamed the Story Bridge Hotel in 1940.

After proving myself to my employer and earning enough credibility, I went from scrubbing dishes to serving customers at the main bar. Having gained some bar experience I went on to other jobs, partly because I just enjoyed living life to the fullest and wanted to experience a lot of things.

During the earliest years of job adventures and living with Mum and Dad, I met a really good guy called Pete. Our friendship came about when my bad attitude became too much for Mum and Dad to bear and they kicked me out of the house.

I guess it didn't help that I had started questioning my belonging, mostly due to my skin colour and ethnicity. Mum and Dad are white Australians, and because I'm Aboriginal by descent, Indigenous to these lands, I identified cultural differences that then led to personality clashes. I'm not going to lie, there were times I struggled to see eye to eye with my sisters and other family members too. Cultural differences played a big part in my feelings.

On the day Mum and Dad kicked me out of the house and told me not to return, I went over to the park across the road from our house. That's when I met Pete. We got talking and one thing led to another. I told Pete my story and he immediately said, "Come live with me at my house," so I did. From that moment forward we became the best of friends, although more like brothers.

The best times of my life were at Pete's house. His parents were cool, successful yet down to earth, and they were fine having me live with them. They gave us free rein to be ourselves. I remember they had a bay cruiser boat that we'd take out and party with mates, we never wanted for anything 'cos Pete's parents had it all.

Pete's mum had earned herself a great career in real estate and excelled in it, achieving a positive reputation amongst property investors and work associates, and Pete's dad owned a nearby pool shop. Two working-class people who had achieved a lot in life, and there I was, an Indigenous black boy who'd been kicked out of home. Nevertheless, Pete's parents welcomed me, accepting me for who I was, skin colour and all. I ended up living with them for approximately twelve months before things changed and it was time to move on.

I went to live with another mate, Nawal, who lived with his dad. His dad was cool and took me in without hesitation. Nawal's mum owned an Indian restaurant and had a unit in Coorparoo. Nawal and I ended up living there, and that's when I found myself working at the Princess Alexandra Hospital for the second time, the very place I had completed my kitchen traineeship.

A year or so later I was able to move out of the Coorparoo apartment, having saved enough money to rent and furnish my own unit in South Brisbane, not too far from the main city. I could finally relax in the space of my abode and began making plans to escape for an overseas holiday. I felt like I needed it because of the many changes I'd put myself through.

Soon enough my holiday was over. An old school mate picked me up from the airport and accompanied me to my home. We weren't expecting to find my place had been ransacked. Someone had broken into the unit, stolen most of my belongings and left me with nothing of value. Seeing how bad the robbery was and knowing my financial situation due to my overseas holiday, my mate kindly offered me a room at his place.

In hindsight, I was distraught about the entire situation. It had taken me a decent amount of time to save up enough money to afford a furnished place, as well as to treat myself to a holiday. Sadly, unexpected life events happen and I simply had to deal with it the way it was.

A little while later, I quit my job at the Princess Alexandra Hospital and moved in with another friend, Nathan, who offered me a job doing prefabrication of sheds. Our living situation didn't last long, despite things going great, as we got told we had to leave because the house we were renting was on crown land and they had other plans.

Luckily, my social circle was big and made up of kind-hearted friends. One of those friends was Brownie. His mum and dad allowed me to live with them, and that lasted for several years. We moved around a lot, living in several different houses in various locations around Brisbane, during which time Brownie and I ended up working with his dad building sheds.

When I eventually moved on from building sheds I went back to the Story Bridge Hotel, where I became the kitchen hand again. Word got out I needed a place and was looking for shared accommodation. A little later I met up with one of the managers and a barmaid, learning we all had things in common. One thing led to another and we ended up sharing a place in New Farm, followed by another place in Coorparoo. A little while after moving to our new place the manager and I ended up having differences. It got so bad I said I'd move out, even though I had nowhere else to go. Sure, my pride got in the way that night, but he wasn't doing things right and I couldn't tolerate his behaviour anymore. Soon enough, one thing led to another and I moved back in with my old mate Pete, down on Tweed Heads, the borderline between QLD and NSW.

I again quit my job at the Story Bridge Hotel and worked at a few local resorts within the vicinity of the Gold Coast. The Gold Coast is popular for resorts, so it made sense for me to get my foot in the door. That only lasted about six months because I started working with Pete in their family pool business. Swimming pools are popular in Queensland) as it's one of the hotter states, reaching high temperatures with variable humidity, often causing bushfires all over the place.

I lived with Pete for almost two years, during which time I stayed working at the pool shop. One of our regular associates was a leak detections expert. We'd talk regularly, but on one occasion he told me he was looking for someone to share his expertise with. Ironically, Pete's dad had recently decided to close the business down, so the timing worked out well. Before long, I was travelling around Brisbane and surrounds learning leak detections and fixing swimming pools.

I was travelling a lot between Tweed Heads and Brisbane and was playing footy all that time. Getting to footy training was becoming a bit of a hassle, so I ended up living in Brisbane again, room-hopping between friends before moving in with one of my two sisters.

Another mate, Paul, who I went to school with, lived across the road from my sister. Paul later helped move my furnishings into Nathan's place at Cleveland. I continued to work around Brisbane doing leak detections and fixing swimming pools, which resulted in me starting my own swimming pool business doing the same thing.

Having been able to save up enough money, I moved from Nathan's house in Cleveland into a rental property of my own, whilst continuing to play football. That's when I became close friends with a lovely woman named Kelli. A little while later, Kelli introduced me to one of her brothers and he offered me a job coal mining in the upper north of Queensland. His offer came at a good time because I needed a change from my current profession, so I accepted and became a coal miner.

The roster was four weeks on, ten days off. I met a guy who ran the local football club not too far from where I was working, and ended up residing in the small-town mining village. After a bit of time passed, differences between friends became apparent and proved difficult to resolve, so I worked for Kelli's other brother, who offered me a job doing maintenance on houses owned by the mines. He was pretty cool and good to work for.

A little while later I moved in with another friend. His neighbour owned a big maintenance company and offered me a different job. So, me being me, I took it. I settled in to the new job quickly. By then footy season had ended, so I had more time available over the weekends.

During one of my work weeks I received a call from my mate Marcus. We'd lived next door to each other back in grade seven. Marcus was getting married, and at short notice invited me to go to his buck's party that weekend at Black Duck, approximately 400 kilometres from where I was working. That didn't stop me from wanting to attend, even though I knew I had ongoing problems with my car.

Friday night after work, I went over to a mate's place to try to fix my car, which then led to a few drinks. Our small social occasion continued into Saturday morning, the day of the buck's party. Another mate mentioned there was a fishing competition in a neighbouring town. I was happy to join them for a short time before heading to Black Duck.

On our way to the fishing competition at Dawson's River, Shawy, Plumber and I called in to the local pub for a few more drinks. We headed out before long, but by the time we got there the boats had already left and the place was deserted, just a few people remaining.

I spotted a rope swing leading over the murky river. Rope swings were popular in my younger years and were on the banks of all the creeks and dams we swam in.

Being the big kid, and wanting to relive childhood memories, I did what most big kids like me would do - I jumped on the rope swing a few times, each time landing in the river. Soon enough, my mates mentioned it was getting late, we needed to leave if we were going to make it to the buck's party on time.

I attempted one last jump - swinging out from the rope swing with a backflip.

Something wasn't right. I began to sink to the river floor. I tried to push myself up using the floor of the riverbed, with no luck. I knew then something was seriously wrong. I was in a lot of trouble.

I had no movement in my arms or my legs. I was underwater, confused, then frantic. I had either landed awkwardly or hit something hard, although I didn't realise it at the time. Unable to move, I couldn't save myself from dying.

That's when I drowned.

My mates soon realised I hadn't resurfaced and jumped in after me. The water was non-transparent, muddy and murky, making their search difficult as they scoured the river to find me. After multiple attempts, my mates were feeling ready to give up when one of them accidentally stood on my arm.

My friends pulled my lifeless body out of the river and proceeded with CPR alongside the riverbank before a lady came over to help. At the time they couldn't find a pulse, apparently there wasn't one.

Thankfully, the woman was able to resuscitate me back to life.

Seconds later, contact was made with the local doctor. He was years into his profession and knew straight away I had broken my neck, with severe spinal cord injuries. Moments later the air ambulance arrived and we were on our way to Rockhampton Hospital, during which time I went into cardiac arrest. They were able to keep me sustained before I underwent a five-and-a-half-hour operation, during which I went into cardiac arrest twice. After that I was placed into an induced coma and airlifted to the Princess Alexandra Hospital where I used to work. In total, I'm told I died five times while undergoing treatment. Overall, the initial operation was of no success, but Dad said I was in God's hands and that God hadn't finished with me yet.

Ironically, and little did I or my parents know it at the time, but I was air travelling over my parents as they drove to Mackay for the arrival of my sister's second son. Dad said they were half an hour away from Mackay when mum got a call on her mobile phone with news that I'd been in an accident. The call cut out. Dad said they got a second call, saying I had been in a bad accident and the call cut out again. When they got to Mackay and were able to get through to the number left on their mobile phone, they finally received the details of the heartbreaking news.

When I arrived at Princess Alexandra Hospital they immediately commenced operating on my neck. Their spinal ward is one of the best. After surgery I fell into a coma for a fair while. When I finally came out of it I could hear, but couldn't move any parts of my limbs. The only movement I had was my eyes. All I could do was blink, and open and close my eyes. God only knows what I was thinking at the time, although I had the feeling my life wasn't going to be the same ever again.

Once I had pulled through my operation and things had settled a little bit, my hospital bed was surrounded by family, friends, doctors and surgeons. The doctors and surgeons were there to check up on me, but also to share devastating life-changing news. They told me I'd never walk or use my arms and legs again, that I was quadriplegic, and the rest of my life would be confined to a wheelchair.

After the Accident

My friends have said they were shocked to see me at the hospital all bright-eyed and bushy-tailed, cracking jokes and laughing almost as if nothing had changed. Some even said they felt sadder than I was. I guess for the most part family and friends struggled to comprehend what had happened to me, but also how it had happened.

But me being me, I just got on with it.

A little while after the experience, having spent two long months in intensive care with complications, setbacks, and one operation after another, things finally began to calm down. I started sharing my life events of having a permanent physical disability throughout schools and local communities, discussing prevention and raising awareness, but also what it feels like to live with spinal cord injuries.

The biggest thing, after accepting the fate that led to the injury and my new destiny, was the frustration of not being able to do things I previously could.

For the most part, we don't realise what we have until it's gone.

My ordinary body movement had gone forever. Getting used to that and accepting it came with a whirl of uncontrollable emotions. But in times of my fate, I just said to myself, "It is what it is, and this is the way I will live the rest of my life, acceptance is key."

Having to move back in with my family after living away for thirteen years was also rather challenging. But over time, and like I had said to myself, you learn to accept things as they are, and then you adjust, eventually working out a way to go on living as independently as you can.

Overall, I haven't let my accident stop me from living a coherent and wholesome life. My life is filled with joy, fun, adventure, love and laughter. I continue to socialise with my mates with regular invitations to parties, concerts and celebrations. My weekdays consist of working from my home office for a local organisation and weekends are often shared with family and close friends. I still catch up with my mate Pete from time to time, travelling down to the Gold Coast occasionally, or he'll come up this way and we'll just hang out. Other friends will call around, bring lunch, say hi, followed by text messages and phone conversations.

In hindsight, life doesn't need to stop because I can no longer walk due to spinal cord injuries. Life stops when we die, and I'm not there yet.

I once was lost, but now I'm found.

Isaiah 53:6

We all, like sheep, have gone astray, each of us has turned to his own way, and the Lord has laid on him the iniquity of us all.

As a result, we can join in praising God for His Amazing Grace and affirm that we were once lost but are now found. Praise God and Thank God.

Hindsight

Regarding my other family on my biological mother's side, I'm the oldest. I have two half-brothers and two half-sisters, each of them with different fathers.

When I reflect on my life and my biological birth family as it is now, they are all criminal people. They've all been in trouble with the law, and each of them has landed themselves in jail.

Thinking about my biological family and the way they have chosen to live, I feel grateful for the cards I've been dealt and the will I have to live. I feel compelled to live an authentic example where I can give back to the people who have given to me, and to the universe for the love I've received.

I am grateful to have been provided with the opportunity to commence a new life with new people, to paramedics, doctors, surgeons, nurses, family and friends - all who have given me hope and provided me with a second chance.

My life expanded in ways that only some can imagine, thanks to my parents.

My family and I have had our differences, but they have loved me in spite of it.

Who would I otherwise be without people who have loved me?

Catastrophe – the realisation for which there is so much to be thankful for.

Everything can change in the blink of an eye, and it did!

What would my life look like if my adoption never took place? Reflection is a good and sure thing. It can also be a sound and solid reminder.

I was once lost and now I've been found.

The greatest healer of all is time.

Sincere and genuine thanks to Mum, Dad, family and friends. I couldn't have done it without each and every one of you.

Appreciation

The road to recovering from life-changing accidents is not always peaceful or harmonious.

Feeling lost, lonely or confused can hit in waves that are huge and overwhelming. Sometimes it's unclear what the right thing to do is, though no one could possibly know what the right thing to do looks like when young, let alone what it means. We can often wonder what we stand for, or what life is supposed to be about. When we are young, we are impartial to all that surrounds us.

We literally float through life with powerlessness, with a sense of desperation that comes out one way or another. When we feel pinned down or knocked over, it's hard to prevent doubts from creeping in and taking over.

- Feeling lost in life can be as painful or exciting as you want to make it. Consequences, on the other hand, can be permanent.
- Fear colours our decisions and makes us act in strange ways in our need to feel less vulnerable. We look for ways to stay busy to distract ourselves from ourselves. When we stop for a moment and reflect over what we are doing, what we have done and why, we don't always like what we see.
- As adults we can all go back to childhood and revisit our younger selves in our younger body, often wondering what we would think. Growing up means starting from zero all over again, admitting to things we had no clue about and admitting to our mistakes that caused us grief. To admit we are clueless about most things in life is a positive step forward and there's absolutely nothing fake about voicing it clearly.
- It's okay to not be okay all of the time, because we are wired that way. We are complex anthropoids and there's no way we could figure everything out in this lifetime.
- We make mistakes and sometimes we end up bounded by them, but that doesn't mean we have to cease living.
- We are never going to be able to fix every situation that happens in our lives. Sometimes we have to accept ourselves the way we are and just enjoy life. And who's to say that anything needs to be fixed? What's happened has happened, sometimes we simply need to accept it and get on with life.

- We get to choose how we look at things. Having a sense of humour can help a lot.
- A lot of what we are all doing isn't really about *what* we are doing, it's more about what's underneath what we are doing.
- If you were to pull back the layers (like you would peel back the husk from the edible part of a banana) what would your life otherwise look like?
- A child thinks an adult has all the answers, that an adult has it all figured out, because that's their overall perspective on things, because that's what they see. As we become more of an adult, we realise that our childlike perspective is far from the truth. Adults, a lot of the time, don't know what to do.
- We should all approach life like a series of experiments.
- It can be exciting to discover ourselves and what we are capable of when pushing through self-limiting boundaries.
- You have to know where you've been to know where you're going.
- When not-so-nice things happen to us, they happen to serve as a catalyst to set things right.

5

Breach of Faith

(Eve, age 45)

Despite coming from a loving home environment growing up, I somehow managed to complicate my entire adult life. I suppose coming from a loving home can do that to you. When you grow up having two parents who love each other to no end, you want the same for yourself because it's part of who you are deep down inside.

Growing up in the '70s was nothing like today. Back then you could do whatever you wanted, as long as you were home by a particular time. People were more relaxed, easy-going and friendly. The world was a lot safer back then too, or so it seemed.

A little while after completing high school I met a guy by chance in a supermarket. Tall, dark and handsome, the kind of guy most girls only dream about, he was polite, courteous and kind. He spoke well and appeared very together, with his dreams and goals very much within reach. We ended up heading to a nearby coffee shop as sparks went flying. On our way there we introduced ourselves by name. I guess we forgot to do that in the heat of initial conversation.

Mason came from a working-class family with a long history of pioneering achievers. They worked hard to maintain their family's work history, ensuring that business aside from family came first. He explained his experience within the family business and that he'd been working alongside his father since a young age. The only thing missing from his life was a beautiful woman.

My dad was a hard-working family man, an engineer who worked at an oil refinery, and Mum was a nurse. We lived in a decent neighbourhood where our neighbours all knew one another and kids and parents from around the neighbourhood would gather for a round of softball, cricket or soccer. Kids were often outside skating the pavements or riding their bikes. Birthday celebrations were a whole lot of fun, we'd have lolly scrambles, play treasure hunt, pin the tail on the donkey, musical chairs, guess-what-food-it-is blind-folded, and guess the song. My childhood life was fun and I remember it well.

After arriving at the café for coffee, Mason and I ended up talking for hours. Coffee turned into lunch, and lunch into an afternoon snack. Realising the time, we knew we had to cut tracks. Mason politely asked for my phone number, then invited me out for dinner the following night. I couldn't resist, so gave him my number and said, "Yes."

I had trouble sleeping that night thanks to the excitement brewing inside.

Emotions were flying high with palpable tingling sensations euphorically overwhelming my body. The next day, I received a phone call from Mason. He explained his excitement for dinner and that he was looking forward to meeting with me again. Mason had booked dinner for 6.30 pm at a popular restaurant minutes before calling me. He asked for my address and said he'd pick me up at 6 pm sharp.

That day couldn't go fast enough. I remember feeling anxious, although quite excited. I spent the day shopping for new clothes because I needed an outfit to wear. The restaurant Mason had chosen was popular for a reason. Dressing up and looking immaculate would be appropriate for the occasion, but more importantly, I felt I needed to look my best.

Mason arrived at 6 pm sharp, just as he'd promised.

After taking our seats and settling in for an evening at dinner together, neither of us could stop staring into each other's eyes, so much so that half the time, I couldn't quite make out what our conversations were actually about. I caught myself day dreaming throughout the night, picturing our future together, and I'm certain Mason was feeling the same way.

All night we smiled, laughed and stared. I was falling for him and he was falling for me too.

After dinner the night was still quite young, so we took a stroll through the city streets, admiring the stars in the night sky. I linked my arm around Mason's and he placed his hand over mine and smiled. He paused and turned to me before leaning in to kiss my lips, then politely asked if I'd be his girlfriend. Without hesitating, I said, "Yes!"

From that night, the throes of love in our relationship escalated fast. There was an unexplainably strong emotional connection that euphorically induced my entire being. I couldn't picture my life without him from that night forward.

Within a short period of time we met with each other's families. Everyone hit it off. Nothing appeared out of the ordinary, just two happy families from slightly different backgrounds coming together and getting along.

Mason was a good listener and took an interest in my life. He was always complimenting me and would communicate with me on a regular basis, sharing his excitement for our future together, and that he wanted to start a family - the sooner the better. Mason often described the life he wanted to live, making his goals evidently clear. He brought a house and immediately said I needed to move in. That was the beginning of the rest of my life.

One thing led to another and soon enough we got married and started making family. Our first child Katelyn was born, making me a housewife. Things were going great with absolutely no complaints. I kept a clean house, did a lot of cooking, did all the washing up, put clothes away, ironed Mason's work pants and shirts, did the gardening, trimmed hedges and mowed lawns, all whilst caring for our daughter. I did everything a good housewife would do. Mason didn't need for anything. By the time Mason arrived home from work dinner was always on the table and the house was never filthy or an untidy mess, our home was always immaculate. I also took good care of myself, ensuring clean eating habits with regular exercise.

Shortly after Katelyn came along we were expecting child number two. Everyone from each of our families was happy for us. This time, as some men do, Mason was hoping for a boy, although it didn't matter if the baby was a girl, the most important thing was the health of the baby. On that note, we decided not to reveal the baby's gender until birth.

Mason was stoked he got his baby boy and together we decided to name him Wyatt. He weighed 8 pounds 5 ounces. After leaving the hospital and settling back into our home, life took on a whole new meaning. Our household became busier than ever with two children to care for, but that didn't prevent me from keeping our house in tip top order. That said, intimate moments with Mason became challenging, especially later in the night when Wyatt would wake and demand feeding. Intimate moments were something we looked forward to, we couldn't keep our hands off one another. The chemistry between us was strong, as was the emotional connection, and whenever we got the chance to make love the inevitable would happen.

After Wyatt's birth our sex life began to slow down a little, although that didn't seem to stop us from falling pregnant a third time. Mason was happy to keep going until we got to baby number five. That's when life took on a whole new meaning and our relationship changed.

One afternoon Rebecca, a close friend of mine, came to visit. Rebecca mentioned she had bumped into Mason with another woman, and although it could've been business, they'd appeared quite close and cosy together.

That afternoon when Mason arrived home, I mentioned that Rebecca had dropped by. Mason immediately said he had bumped into her during a lunch meeting with a new business associate, and explained that he had hired a female to help improve the company's brand. I thought nothing of it, but as the weeks went on, Mason started arriving home later than usual, which led to late-night arguments. Arguments eventually turned violent. For the first time in our marriage he hit me across the face. I can't remember what I said to provoke his rage, however I do remember Mason apologising and immediately saying he'd never hit me again.

A few months went by and Mason was still arriving home late. I asked time and time again if our marriage was in trouble, if so, we needed to repair whatever issues we were having. Mason claimed our marriage didn't need repairing, that everything was fine and I was just overreacting. The next day I thought about what Mason had said. Perhaps I was overreacting, after all, being a housewife was starting to take a toll on me with five children to love and care for and a big house to maintain. Maybe we just needed a break, some time alone with one another.

When Mason finally arrived home and had settled in for the night I tried making love to him, but he didn't feel like it. He explained his exhaustion from work. I mentioned we needed some time alone together and that a couple of nights away without the kids would be of benefit to us. Mason refused, saying he had way too much work to get through and now wouldn't be a good time. His behaviour went on for weeks and arguments became frequent, as did the violent abuse. He'd attack me time and time again, telling me to shut up about his late arrivals and that if I didn't like it, just leave. But leaving wasn't that easy because I loved him with all my heart. I couldn't see my life without Mason, and my love for our family was all I had at the time. I didn't know anything else, and in all honesty, I was co-dependent on Mason financially.

Our families never knew about our marriage problems or the violence within it. I hid it from my parents and his. I couldn't help but love Mason, despite how he treated me. I continued to see the good in him and he never laid a hand on the children, nor did the children see us argue, unless of course they could hear us. That said, our arguments wouldn't last long and when he'd hit me there was no more to be said.

The only person I confided in was Rebecca. I knew I could trust her, and I needed an outlet, someone to talk with and vent to.

A year or so later, and feeling like a battered housewife, I found incriminating and intimate text messages on Mason's mobile phone. The use of mobile phones became popular in the early 1990s, and text messaging took on a whole new meaning in the late 1990s.

I confronted Mason, who eventually came clean about his indiscretion and late arrivals home. He said he'd been having an affair with the woman he employed and that she wasn't the only woman he had slept with over the past year or more. Within seconds my heart broke. I felt intimately betrayed. How could anyone say they love and care for someone and then lie to them like that?

At first, I didn't want to believe what I was hearing, but Mason confessed. The floor beneath my feet started to crumble. I fell into a bottomless chasm, an absolute abyss, with nothing left to hold on to. My reality had vanished in an instant, my entire future rewritten. I felt completely and utterly lost.

When I finally got time to reflect on my life as it was, I couldn't seem to justify the sacrifices I had made just to please Mason. I loved him so much I had forgotten to love myself in the process. When Mason told me of his infidelity issues a whirl of emotions hit me like a tonne of bricks. I felt train-wrecked, like the biggest loser, a complete reject and a lone-ranger on a dark and emotional rollercoaster ride. Mason lying to me was the biggest betrayal, and I wasn't sure how I was going to forgive him.

I wasn't sure if I was willing to overlook his confession or sacrifice our relationship due to his infidelity. There was no denying my love for Mason, I loved him with every ounce of my body. Deciding what to do wasn't simple, even amongst my devastation.

The thought of my marriage falling apart prompted a sense of humiliation and shame. Somewhere amongst all I was feeling, emptiness and the loss of affection for someone I loved set a shadow over my entire being. For weeks I questioned what went wrong. I started blaming myself for not knowing the truth. I felt annoyed, irritated, and angry with myself.

How could I have let this happen? How did I not know it was happening? All the obvious warning signs were there. Where was my womanly intuition? How could I have failed to pick up on subtle changes that pointed directly to infidelity? Was I so blinded by the truth that I didn't want to admit it to myself?

Realising my husband had cheated on me raised a slew of insecurities. Over time, I started hating myself for not knowing, reflecting heavily on things I thought I had done wrong to drive Mason to cheat on me. I'd mull over my dreams, which included the family we had created together as a married couple. Then reality hit home - what dreams? My hopes and dreams had been shattered due to my husband's infidelity, and in that notion, I came down hard on myself for being blind. Sadness turned into depression; depression led me to a dark place of wanting to commit suicide. The only thing that prevented me from doing so was my love for my children.

My ability to rebuild trust in my husband proved problematic as I had a difficult time trying to overcome the betrayal. Mason's cheating was hurtful enough, his lying about it added other elements of betrayal. Mason admitting to it was a crucial factor that I deliberated over for months, but sadly it didn't change the way I felt, nor did it make the pain go away. I also didn't want to become someone I wouldn't like. If my best self could no longer show up in my relationship with Mason, what would be the point?

Infidelity can create crippling side-effects on self-worth. It can also drive constant questioning about whether your partner is likely to cheat again, which makes it hard to put what happened to you behind you.

Choosing to end a marriage is never easy, especially when children hold a forever bond with the one you completely and utterly love. Deep down, I just knew our relationship wouldn't bode well for the future. I needed to save myself from further emotional damage and get on with rebuilding my life with my children.

Moving On

Recovering from infidelity means discovering a new sense of self. Surrounding yourself with people who love and support you makes the journey easier.

- Like a head injury, sometimes life experiences can leave you feeling lost, confused and disoriented. Even through times of recuperation, mind senses can remain partially disabled.
- Eyesight is like hindsight: If eyesight is blurry, so is hindsight. Blurred vision will jar your equilibrium.
- I have stumbled and I have fallen, though I have stumbled upon self-worth.
- If I am unable to care for my children, who other than their mother will care for them?

- There are always going to be unsettling side effects in decisions we make. There is no greater feeling than the value of self-worth.
- During my senseless periods in life, I went through emotions of *why me, why this, why now?* Make no mistake—God is real.
- Downtime and reflection are perfect opportunities to enable changes that will enhance your life.
- Thy shall not allow my sense of motherhood, my sense of place, my sense of purpose, my sense of safety, my sense of peace and my sense of self-worth to be erased.
- Move on, even at the risk of sounding or showing callousness.
- I refuse to let negative life experiences define me.
- Divinity can be found where and when you least expect it.
- We don't know how blessed we are until misfortune strikes. Sometimes misfortune needs to happen more than once.
- In every life lesson there is something valuable to learn.
- Through the power of life lessons, we can discover the grace of gratitude.
- Moving on isn't always easy, but the results from doing so are rewarding.

6
Household Chambers

(Lea, age 30)

My parents broke up when I was about four years old. I was seven when my mother's boyfriend began to sexually abuse me.

Mum was a drug addict and Dad was an alcoholic. I grew up in a low socio-demographic area where most households were poor, unemployed and living off welfare benefits while living in Housing Commission homes. Households struggled day-to-day to keep up with bills and put food on the table. People struggled to keep their heads above water, yet seemed to have enough to feed their illicit habits.

There was no shame in our neighbourhood. People argued on the streets and did all kinds of ungodly acts in public. Lawns were overgrown, mail boxes were destroyed or beaten up by vandals, and some houses looked like junk yards while others looked abandoned, even though they were lived in. People literally had no pride or self-respect. Though young at the time and outwardly impartial to my surroundings, I think, deep down, I kind of knew there was more to life than the neighbourhood I lived in.

I rarely saw my dad after he and Mum broke up. In fact, we didn't have a father-daughter relationship after that. Mum started seeing other guys. Her relationships never lasted long and they were typically low-lifes – deadbeat boyfriends going nowhere fast.

Later down the track, Mum found a more stable relationship with a guy she met at the local pub. A regular drinker, he would often wake up with a beer in his hand after being in a drunken stupor the night before. He rarely held down a job, freeloading off government handouts. To my disgust, freeloading appeared an easy option for him, especially since he received just enough to feed his drinking habit.

When I left for school in the mornings he was always on the couch drinking beer, and when I returned after school he'd still be on the couch, drinking beer and watching TV. He never seemed to help around the house. Mum did all the work, although it wasn't much. Mum wasn't interested in my life, it was almost as if I didn't exist and wasn't there. I grew up quickly, learning independence at an early age, knowing if I didn't do it myself, no one else would.

One night, Mum's boyfriend came into the bathroom while I was relaxing in the bath tub. He was drunk and disorderly, no surprise there, yet managed to stare at me long enough to make me feel uncomfortable. That was the beginning of his grooming behaviours.

Mum left me at home with him on various occasions. I was scared and didn't trust him one bit. I'd ask Mum if I could go with her, but she'd often say no, leaving me at home with him. Sometimes I'd try locking myself in my room, but my bedroom door handle was loose, then over time, it was rendered useless, completely broken. The door handles throughout the house were the same. I'd stuff the door holes with old clothes for privacy, and sometimes I'd use a kitchen chair or a kitchen knife to keep the door securely closed.

One day Mum's boyfriend pushed my bedroom door open because I forgot to secure it with a knife or kitchen chair. He tried talking to me, but every word fell on deaf ears because I felt anxious and fearful of him. My gut instinct said not to trust him, and I didn't, he was creepy.

Over a period of time, his grooming became more intense. I tried to tell Mum on various occasions, but she was so wasted and high on drugs that nothing I said sunk in.

Then one night he snuck into my room while Mum was passed out on the couch in the living room. He slipped into my bed, waking me up by fondling me. He ran his hands over my body, touching my private parts and whispering not to tell my mum. I was scared and wanted to scream, but I was paralysed. Moments later he left. I forced myself back to sleep in the hope I'd simply wake to find it was just a bad dream.

The next day after school, when I was finally able to get mum alone, I tried to tell her about it yet again, only this time she heard me, though she refused to believe me. My safety and wellbeing were of no concern to her. I knew I was on my own and had to fend for myself after that. She was only interested in one thing, and that was getting herself wasted again, often preoccupied with figuring out how to get her next fix.

Several days after the first incident he sexually abused me again. It soon became a routine for him. He would finger my vaginal area. I remember feeling his erect penis stabbing me in the back of my thighs. He'd try to insert his penis between my tightly closed legs for penetration and to make himself orgasm. I hated him for it and I knew it was wrong, but after a while of consistent fondling I found myself enjoying the unknown sensation, one I had not experienced before. The next day I'd feel emotionally low yet sexually high, then I'd feel sick to my stomach about it.

The abuse went on for almost three years, until I grew the courage to speak up at school. I told friends first, who encouraged me to tell the teacher. The school principal and counsellors got involved, social welfare services were called and Mum was told to come down to the school. A short while later the police arrived.

I don't remember much after that point, although social services were heavily involved in my life thereafter. That's when I was placed in foster care, going from household to household. I felt lost, alone, angry and confused.

One day I was placed with a family who lived in a medium to high decile area. This meant I lost my community, my school and my friends. Everything I had ever known was removed from my life. My new foster carers enrolled me in a school that was nothing like my old school, where my inclination to withdraw emotionally on account of the sexual abuse made it difficult to make new friends.

It took me approximately eighteen months to finally settle in with my new foster parents. They were a lot older than my mum. I think at the time they would've been in their late forties or early fifties. They had looked after a number of kids who had suffered trauma at an early stage in life. They became my long-term carers, people who encouraged me to live my best life. They were good people, but I still missed and loved my mum.

The initial transition into foster care was difficult, but after living a while with long-term foster carers who showed love in meaningful ways, I couldn't help but grow a liking toward them, and deep down I knew if social services sent me back to live with my mum I'd be back where I started. Somehow, I understood that people like Mum rarely change, and her sick, perverted boyfriend was better off in prison.

When I look back on my experiences as a child, I often wish I was better prepared. I used to wish I was strong enough to fight for myself so as to avoid the entire sexual assault ordeal. I would wish Mum was a different person and that Dad had stuck around. I learnt to stop wasting my time wishing for a different past and started praying for a better future instead.

My foster carers were warm, welcoming, sensitive and loving people. I felt myself blossom in their care. But after several months, the difficulties of my past manifested into sadness, followed by depression. My foster carers' unfailing support couldn't reach me, and at the age of almost fourteen I tried to commit suicide. I cut my wrist, hoping to bleed to death. My foster mum found me and immediately called for an ambulance. The hospital placed me under surveillance. Suicide watch, they called it.

In amongst my foster carers' devastated emotions and my awakening, they were there for me. They rarely left my side, telling me they loved me more than words could describe. For the first time in their care, I sobbed a little, and then I cried. Tears poured heavily from my eyes, like a fountain out of control. For the first time in my life, I communicated my bottled-up feelings from inside. I spoke openly to my carers about what had happened to me as a child. I explained the amount of shame, guilt and embarrassment I'd been harbouring and that suicide was my way out. They were both attentive, supportive and understanding. They offered reassurance that things would get better and advised appropriate treatment would be made available as soon as I was feeling better and was ready to accept it.

My foster carers were good people. They were always true to their words.

Previous foster carers didn't show much respect or love toward me, and there was hardly any privacy in their homes. But my new foster carers showed me love, with relenting persistence that the past needn't be the case in their home. They were there for me every step of the way and showed me things I wouldn't have otherwise learnt. They would tell me they were not there to replace my mum that my mum loved me even though I felt she didn't because of the shit she put me through.

During my years of maturity, I would question my life. I'd ruminate about my childhood and try to come up with preventatives, sometimes contemplating various 'what ifs.' That said, ruminating and contemplating often led to self-blame. I'd begin to hate myself for feeling a certain way or being a certain way, and for allowing my mother's perverted boyfriend to take advantage of me. I'd question myself, asking *why me? Why did he have to sexually abuse me? Why not make love to my mother or some woman his own damn age?*

Further rumination would lead me to question my mother's integrity. Why wouldn't she believe my story? Why would my mother deny responsibility over me? How could she not feel guilty about leaving me alone with her drunken, deadbeat boyfriend? Why hasn't she apologised? Is she ever going to apologise? Can she not see how this traumatising event has affected, embroiled and implicated my life?

How do I forgive Mum for allowing a bad, life-changing traumatic event to happen to her child? How does a young child deal with such a horrible experience and overcome the trauma of it? As an adult, how do you forgive your mother for turning a blind eye to her child being sexually assaulted by her own boyfriend?

No matter how many years go by, anyone who has ever been sexually abused as a child suffers. The memories are there forever. Truth is, I have built a love-hate relationship with my mother. She is impossible to replace, despite her many faults and the same old illicit habits, I'm still learning to forgive her.

Fortunately, my experience with my long-term foster carers was amazing. God was looking out for me and purposely placed me with two very loving people who never gave up on me, despite my mood swings, my attempt at suicide and depressive feelings.

The most valuable life lesson I learned from my foster care experience is to never give up on a child, even when they upset and sadden you. Children need time, love, support and energy to get them on the right track. I know as a child I did a lot of stupid things and I put my foster carers through a tonne of heartache, but they loved me no matter what I did, and they made sure I was aware of that.

Sadly, we don't always read good news about foster carers, but I was fortunate to experience life within a normal and loving household for a while. I am grateful.

Forgiveness

Trauma and pain can lead to health and wellbeing issues. Sadly, for some forgiveness doesn't come easily.

Forgiveness is freedom. Forgiving people who have hurt us sets us free.

We can all benefit immensely when we learn to forgive those who have hurt us. Forgiveness enables you to fulfil future hopes as well as your true potential. Forgiveness allows you to break free from limiting beliefs and attitudes, and from heavy thought patterns and emotionally draining energies so you can apply yourself towards creating the life you always wanted. Forgiveness allows you to create well-designed pathways that will improve your everyday living, helping you to reach your most practical and immediate goals you set for yourself.

When we don't forgive, we trap unwanted energies inside our bodies, limiting ourselves from wondrous growth that can catapult us forward with tremendous velocity. Anyone needing to remove unwanted energies would sooner forgive than hold on to resentment, because they know what's good for them deep down inside.

An emotionally trapped life isn't a life at all, so forgiveness is the only key to happiness.

If you decide forgiveness isn't the answer and you choose to continue feeling entrapment, the choices you make and the things you believe will all be influenced by ways you've not forgiven. Decisions are likely to be based on resentment, dislike and negativity, and in turn will result in adverse and unfavourable outcomes.

If you do not want to learn forgiveness for yourself, the least you can do is learn to forgive for the benefits of others.

When you're ready to learn forgiveness, you become more open to success in whatever ways are meaningful to you, and your thinking becomes clear and positive.

When you learn forgiveness, all that seemed impossible becomes possible and achievable.

When you learn to forgive, abilities that are dormant within you will emerge. You will then discover within yourself a stronger and more capable person than you previously imagined. You will learn to let go off struggles and begin to thrive.

Overcoming Core Wounds Within Us

Memories can be painful. They can evoke old wounds that represent dark periods in our lives. Our more torturous memories can leave indelible marks deep inside the soul, causing us to believe we are unworthy of happiness, pleasure, love and fulfilment. Though core wounds vary according to our circumstances and experience, deep fundamental wounds are the result of fundamental beliefs that we have either witnessed or learnt from childhood, and they contribute to the faulty self-image we carry around in our adult life.

Dysfunction in family is where conflict and instability are common. While no family is perfect, real dysfunction may only become evident when adverse behaviours make it difficult for individual family members to function, thrive, and grow into human beings who can flourish.

If dysfunction causes you to distance yourself from family rather than build up emotions focused on hate, that's perfectly okay. We often love our family, but that doesn't necessarily mean we like them or enjoy being around them. There's an adage that's been around for centuries, 'blood is thicker than water.' While this is known to be true, not everyone shares the same perspective on it.

Looking at things from a different perspective allows us to create new perceptions. For example: While blood is thicker than water, blood stains, and some stains are difficult to remove. Though we cannot re-write the past, we can prioritise aspirations and create a successful and fulfilling end.

Turning towards science, we know water hydrates and is obviously very good for us. It's the same for quality friendships. Dysfunctional families are often known to bring us down, whereas quality friendships raise us up. The moral of the story is that blood stains, but water hydrates our being and quenches our thirst for life.

It is important to surround yourself with like-minded people who are willing to add joy to your life, as you would theirs.

Core wounds are extremely varied and diverse. The trauma inflicted during the earliest years of life can alter a child's molecular biology, which can lead to a life of serious mental and physical maladies.

Core wounds are often made up of the following:
- Abandonment at a young age.
- Childhood neglect.
- Sexual, physical, mental and emotional abuse.
- Incestuous relationships.
- Rape, date rape, gang rape, statutory rape, prison rape, payback rape.
- Rejection.
- Betrayal.
- Manipulation.
- Overbearing parent figure.
- Malicious family members.

The stress of trauma in the earliest stages of life is known to cause changes to our cell structure, leading later in life to:

- Eating disorders.
- Substance abuse.
- Paranoia.
- Disruptive neurodevelopment.
- Cognitive impairment.
- Anxiety.
- Chronic fatigue syndrome.
- Depression.
- High blood pressure.
- Chronic inflammation.
- Hypertension.
- Heart disease.
- Cancer.

Trauma of any kind is long-lasting and is the result of human deficiencies; whereby it explicitly creates false beliefs systems that enable convictions and judgements that define our sense of self. False beliefs systems determine how we feel about others or how happy we are within ourselves, and how we perceive the world to be. False beliefs systems are also responsible for how successful or not we are, creating disillusionment of our dreams before we even begin to try. That is when we become confused and lose our sense of direction in life. It happens, and sometimes it happens to those who don't appear to have suffered significantly or immensely, for losing direction is all part of living.

When it comes to fixing our life from the outside in, truth is, it's an extremely limited pathway and will only get us so far. We can look after ourselves by changing our eating habits, taking better care of our bodies, our skin and the environment we live in. Changing all these habits brings short-lived good feelings, and feeling miserable again is inevitable because the real work hasn't even begun. But it's got to get worse before it gets better.

After changing several lifestyle habits, expect to continue feeling miserable. Expect to continue torturing yourself with shame, guilt, self-pity and self-destructive behaviours that make you feel as though you're back to square one, and yes you are. That said, there is hope for all of us, no matter the destination reached.

The journey itself may seem bleak, but the journey thereafter will help to eradicate the undesirable at heart. The next step forward involves taking a brand-new approach.

The new path starts within you first.

It starts at the heart of the issue, the root core embedded in you. It's a difficult path to travel, but is ultimately rewarding because it helps put an end to your self-imposed suffering.

When you begin this new journey, you must prepare yourself for a significant amount of discomfort. You must be willing to face the whole truth and nothing but the truth, even if you know you're not going to like it. Remember, there's nothing to like about the violation of trauma, but facing every inch of reality related to your trauma will help you uncover the kingpin of your pain.

When you finally uncover the kingpin, you will learn that manipulation is not only a huge hindrance, it is also killing your spirit, mind, body and soul. Don't let your core beliefs produced from trauma manipulate your perception. Instead, take a fire torch and set fire to manipulation and let it all go.

Here are examples of what you will set fire to and let go of. Each of these are part of false beliefs produced by a diverse range of trauma:

- I'm not good enough.
- I am unlovable.
- I don't deserve love.
- Nobody likes me, everyone hates me.
- The world is against me.
- I am worthless.
- I'm a loser, I've achieved nothing in my life.
- I have nothing going for my life.
- I'm not talented enough.
- I'm too stupid to excel in life.
- I'm a failure to myself, my children and my family.
- I don't matter, my life doesn't matter.
- I have no hope, there is no hope.
- My problems in life can't be solved.
- I don't deserve good things to happen to me.
- I am unwanted and invisible to most people.
- I am shameful.
- I will die alone.
- My life was a mistake.
- My parents never loved me. I don't even love myself.
- I am ashamed of what happened to me, even though it wasn't my fault.
- I blame myself for my life happenings.

False belief systems are detrimental to our lives and disable any chance of happiness and fulfilment. When we repeatedly talk to ourselves in this manner we believe these things to be true, when really, they're far from the truth and create an endless array of psychological health issues.

To help you overcome false beliefs created from the trauma that repeatedly beat you to your knees, destroying your spiritual wellbeing and robbing you from feeling whole, here are beneficial ways to help with your fight against negativity.

Write Down Each False Belief That Impacts Your Life, and Work at Each Slowly

It is counterproductive to try to solve every false belief you've identified all at once, so start working on them one at a time. You are likely to discover at least one or more persistent false beliefs you'll need to eliminate prior to tackling each of the others.

Acknowledge how Each False Belief Impacts or Thwarts Your Life

To make concrete, life-changing steps forward, you must truly understand what impacts your everyday life, and furthermore your life as a whole.

For example: You might question how the identified false belief impacts your life, and therefore, you might answer it in this way:

> This identified false belief impacts my life in a way that I don't feel worthy or deserving. It stops me from feeling confident. It makes me anxious in

public. It makes me feel sad, causing me to feel hurt
or displaced most of the time. It makes me doubt
myself, and then I start to hate myself because of it.
It causes me to fail in everything I give my heart to.
It causes me to eat more, where I begin to treat my
body like a garbage bin. I treat my loved ones the
same way I treat myself, which isn't good.
I don't feel great about it and I end up punishing
myself over it. When I look in the mirror all I see
is worthlessness and ugliness triggering memories
of the past that I wish were never there.

While false beliefs may sound ridiculous to some, they are real to others, and sadly they wreak havoc over people's lives because of the intensity of realism attached to false beliefs.

It's imperative to rate each false belief to its significance.

For example: Rate each false belief between 1 and 10.
1 represents: Not so significant or harmful.
10 represents: Negatively significant and harmful.

Strength of Your False Beliefs

Not so significant or harmful.									Negatively Significant and harmful.
1.	2.	3.	4.	5.	6.	7.	8.	9.	10.
O	O	O	O	O	O	O	O	O	O

Now write down another score rating system using the numbers 1 to 10 and ask yourself how strongly you believe each of these to be true.

1 represents: I don't believe it at all.
10 represents: I strongly believe this to be true.

I don't believe it at all.							I strongly believe this to be true		
1.	2.	3.	4.	5.	6.	7.	8.	9.	10.
O	O	O	O	O	O	O	O	O	O

Results will vary for everyone, though in general you'll be able to determine a level of emotion and the impact of that emotion, even if you were to reverse the score rating above.

Now you have determined a result for each score rating, for example, maybe you scored from number 6 and upwards. If this is the case, the overall happiness and fulfilment score rating will provide a bigger window of hope for change, mostly because you are sad more than you are happy, proving false beliefs systems are a detriment to your life.

If this is the case, the overall happiness and fulfilment score rating will look something like this:

☺				😐					☹
1.	2.	3.	4.	5.	6.	7.	8.	9.	10.
○	○	○	○	○	○	○	○	○	○

When you score greater than 6 you will see the overall impact created by trauma that has led you down a pathway of false beliefs.

Next: Question why you Believe Relentless False Beliefs to be True

Perhaps in your childhood you were told time and time again by an adult that you were useless. Maybe you've heard family members frequently criticise you, which made you believe those words, and it's stuck with you ever since. Maybe family members would run you down, talk down to you or speak negatively towards you, making you feel bad about yourself. You might have been beaten up, victimised, mentally, emotionally, physically and sexually abused, and as a result of trauma you've built false beliefs about yourself over a long period of time.

Write down your memories or experiences that uphold false beliefs and explore hidden forms of resistance.

For example: Write down significant events that have taken place in your life. By doing so, you are creating a narrative that helps you understand how you became you. If you are not thrilled about how events in your life have worked out, find time to reflect over events in a thoughtful way. Doing so will allow you to understand your life in a more meaningful way.

If you scored less than 5, try to identify emotions, such as fear, that could be hiding behind false beliefs.

Explore Forms of Resistance

There are many reasons why we consciously or unconsciously refuse to change our core beliefs, regardless of whether they are true or false. Our reasons often involve fear of failure, fear of change, and fear of uncertainty. If you have been habituated to think and behave in a particular way all your life, what would happen if you chose otherwise? What would happen if you changed habitual behaviours and created brand new ones?

Before changing habitual thinking patterns that have led to false beliefs, you need to make sure you can deeply commit to the journey.

Finding Ways to Debunk Habitual Thinking Patterns That Create False Beliefs

Finding ways to debunk false beliefs will prove to your unconscious mind that you are no longer willing to allow habitual thinking patterns to negatively impact your life. At some point throughout this journey of change, you will consciously commit yourself by saying inwardly that you are ready to let go of deeply held convictions that no longer serve a purpose for your life.

The pillar of meaning is belonging: Value others and find people who value you.

Relationships where you are valued for who you intrinsically are, and where you value others with the same elemental connection, is a clear example of sharing interpersonal relationships of unique bonds.

Life without purpose is a body without a soul.
The meaning of life is to find your gift.
The purpose of life is to give it away.

Pablo Picasso

The key to purpose is using your strengths to serve others. In other words, find your gift and put it to good use. Purpose gives you something to live for, it provides you with a reason to move forward. It's our reason for existing and drives us to accomplish various achievements throughout our entire life.

Find your purpose and allow the streams of fulfilment to flood the gates of life wholesomely and rightfully.

Transcendent states are rare moments for everyone. When you feel a state of transcendence, you'll feel lifted from daily responsibilities and connect to a higher reality. It's an experience that feels larger than life, though different people will feel transcendence in different ways. To paint a basic picture of transcendence: You'll find yourself in a zone where you lose the sense of time, space and place.

False beliefs cripple us, imprison us, slow us down and hold us back. They carry a significant amount of weight over our life that restrains us from moving forward and getting on with it. False beliefs prevent us from relishing in joy and block our true passage to living authentically and intrinsically. They hold us back from being who we really are and what we ultimately deserve in life. False beliefs are fallacious, flawed, unfounded and extremely unrealistic. That is why we need to replace them.

How to Change from False Beliefs to Positive Core Beliefs

Identify what false beliefs you have. Maybe you focus too much time on what you look like, rather than who you really are. When we live in vanity, we fixate too much of our time toward looking good, rather than fixing what doesn't spiritually feel right within us. We may look good on the surface, but deep down resides an absence of Trinity in our souls. That's why it's important to choose core beliefs that positively impact and change our life.

Positive core beliefs enable us to move with purpose and provide meaning over our life. As a result, we feel emotionally fulfilled. Positive core beliefs enable joy, confidence and creativity, and allow us to let go of toxic behaviours, including false beliefs that have prevented us from shining all of this time.

Remember, happiness comes and goes. When life is good, it's good, but when things are bad or life goes pear-shaped, having meaning and purpose will give you something to hold on to.

Afterword

You made it to the end! Congratulations and thank you for your attention.

Now that you've read through this book, what are some of the things you are looking for?

Are you able to spot someone who's experienced trauma or is going through a difficult time in life?

When it comes to trauma, one of the first things you can look for in someone is changes. For example, someone who used to be outgoing is now isolative, or someone who used to be happy-go-lucky is now sad or anxious. Maybe their health has deteriorated overnight, with consistent complaints of tummy aches, headaches, or maybe they're purposely taking days off school or work. Maybe they're self-harming, pulling out their own hair, cutting, biting or burning.

People with depression usually have problems sleeping, or sleep too much. They can also go through various changes in appetite, where they become so anxious that they don't want to eat, or they'll self-medicate, causing them to overeat.

Depressed people may choose to indulge in alcohol or illicit drugs. Sometimes they'll show signs of continuous absenteeism from work, or they'll overwork themselves, becoming a workaholic. These are all signs that someone is suffering, and it doesn't always have to relate to trauma. They are, however, sure signs someone is going through change in life and may not be coping effectively.

The word trauma can be confusing because it literally has three definitions. The first definition relates to a damaged mind that occurs as a result of distressing psychological experiences. Psychological trauma is often the result of overwhelming stress that exceeds our coping mechanism and generally robs a person of any joy.

The second relates to physical injury that results in physical trauma to the body, such as broken bones, wounds, or internal organ damage. People who experience physical trauma may also experience psychological difficulty due to the shock of the unexpected injury.

Trauma can also link to grief, though it is not quite the same as the first two. Instead, it is an emotional response to a surprising and terrible event, such as the loss of a loved one.

While trauma is different for everyone, two of the more common reactions are feeling strongly about something or not feeling much at all.

If you've been through trauma and you've reached a point in life that enables you to search for answers, the first step in dealing with trauma is to acknowledge the trauma and accept that your emotions have been affected by it. After that you can reach out and seek help from professionals, although caring family members or friends can also be helpful.

I sincerely hope this book provides enriching life experiences that add meaning and value to your life, that you are able to relate to traumatic life-changing experiences in your own way, and that it provides clarity on things you are in search of.

I hope this book triggers a list of self-enquiring questions to enlarge the window of hope as you turn back the hands of time to start a clean slate, enabling you to adopt behavioural strategies and develop brand new core beliefs. May you find moments where you can look beyond life's broken bits and adversities and see what a difference changing your thought patterns creates.

Pledge to be stigma-free and live the life you know you deserve.

Yours sincerely,
Tina Agassiz

Acknowledgements

There are many people present in my life who deserve credit, though the ones who deserve credit the most are the ones who have consistently supported this book from beginning to end.

I extend my sincerest appreciation and deepest gratitude to my partner, Paul Bravey. Thank you for taking a sincere interest in the development of my lifelong dream as I dedicate my talent to serve others, and for understanding my change of moods throughout the journey of writing this book and realising the depth of my soul.

A warm and genuine thanks to particular family members for supporting this journey from the very beginning, starting with my first book *Eclectic Afflatus*: Pania Kingi, Norman McGregor, Jason Smith, Kathryn Levaillant, Hare Kingi, Janie Kingi, Joshua and Kerri Vaka, Lisa Gillette and Gillian Gillette.

Furthermore, a heartfelt thanks for the ongoing encouragement, love and support from ever lasting friendships: George Drollett, Brendon Roy, Leigh Ann Levy, Graham Weatherhog, Donna Burns, Tessa Green, Ngawai Gerrard, Herb Ratahi, Mark Simpson, Daniel Quinlan, Pam McInnes, Sally Poona and Jay Tarawhiti of Queensland, Australia.

Darcel Manihera of Melbourne, Australia.

Elizabeth Stuart, Clayton Kelly, Zane Reagon, Pouya Bakhspour Charlie and Mercedez Saba, Nourah and George

Saba, Jonas Chung, Grace Marie, Brad Nathan, Armani Pedisic, Anna Crosato of Sydney, Australia.

Neil Permain of Perth, Western Australia.

Ray Stephens, Esther Edmonds, Chris Edmonds, Bijanni Aspinall and Shake Ram of New Zealand.

I extend warm thanks to consistent Facebook followers: Tyra Francis, Lisa Smith and Samantha Paterson from the United Kingdom. Heather Bueltemann, Jean Brown, Lauren Perry, Scott Brown, Ace Ramos, Melissa Conquest, Kelly O'Connor, Della Bicknell, Mary Ann Merryman Knott, Kathleen Cantey and Angie Butler from the United States of America. Erina Praise of Uganda and Martin King of Spain.

Thank you, Massey Joy Wardens of Zambia, for your input, knowledge and kind and loving heart.

A sincere thank you to my publishing provider who've provided hands on support of this project, and a special thank you to Karen Collyer, my editor.

To my children Kaelyn and Sidon for independently living their lives knowing how tough life is, through observing and understanding my nature and placement in this world.

The service to others is a way of life and provides meaning to human existence. Your achievements in life bring joy to my life and I'm so happy for each of you.

Finally, I'd like to express my deepest gratitude to my beloved grandmother, Margaret, for loving me during childhood and seeing something special within me when others did not.

Surely someone may find certain lapses and deficiencies in this book, there is room for improvement everywhere we look.

CPSIA information can be obtained
at www.ICGtesting.com
Printed in the USA
LVHW080543031121
702323LV00008B/367

9 780648 997900